Zinnia AND THE BEES

DANIELLE DAVIS

STONE ARCH BOOKS
a capstone imprint

Zinnia and the Bees is published by Stone Arch Books
1710 Roe Crest Drive
North Mankato, Minnesota 56003
www.mycapstone.com

Library of Congress Cataloging-in-Publication Data is available on the
Library of Congress website.

ISBN 978-1-4965-4661-6 (library binding)
ISBN 978-1-62370-867-2 (paper over board)
ISBN 978-1-62370-868-9 (reflowable epub)

Summary: While Zinnia's seventh-grade classmates are celebrating the last
day of school, she's stuck serving detention for yarn bombing a statue of
the school mascot. And when she rushes home to commiserate with her
older brother and best friend, Adam, she's devastated to discover that he's
left home with no explanation. Just when it looks like Zinnia's day can't
possibly get any worse, a colony of frantic honeybees mistakes her hair for a
hive and lands on her head!

Designers: Tracy McCabe / K.Fraser
Cover and interior illustrations: Laura Horton

Additional cover images: Shutterstock:
Boogie Man (honey drips), Peter Walters (bees)

Printed and bound in China.
010339F17

For Todd

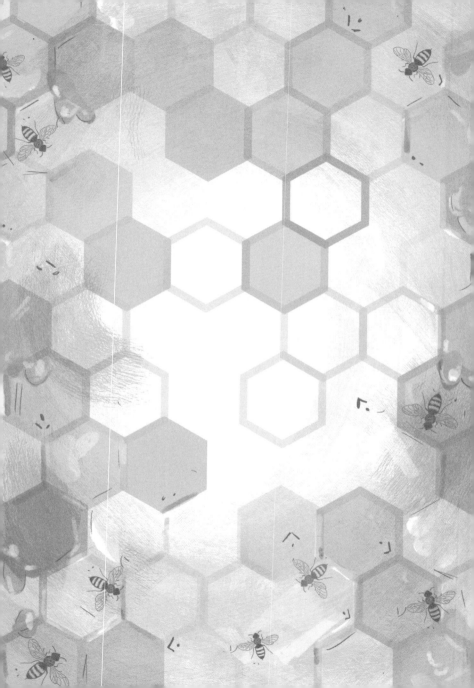

1
OPERATION YARN BOMB

Ronny the Rattlesnake is naked.

But not for long.

"Adam, meet Ronny," I say, motioning to the three-foot-tall rattlesnake statue — my middle school mascot — in front of us. I'm the only one who calls him Ronny. As far as I know, I'm the only one who calls him anything at all. I decided a while back that Ronny needed a name *and* an outfit. Today he'll finally get the outfit part.

My older brother inspects the statue and gives Ronny's metal tail a shake hello. "Zin, this yarn bomb is going to be the best ever," he says.

On Adam's scale of things being great, *best ever* is the highest. The very best. And Adam's never been wrong.

Most of the neighborhood isn't even awake yet in the muddy pre-dawn light. It's five-thirty in the morning, the last day before summer vacation, and as planned, Adam and I are the only ones at school. We're dressed in dark colors for our secret operation. I wear charcoal gray, like always, and Adam wears all black — except for his blue boots, which he practically never takes off.

"Ready?" I ask.

Adam crinkles his eyebrows, making his face look way more serious than usual, and nods. Then he unzips the retro duffel bag he's carrying and holds it open in my direction before swiveling his head around to keep watch.

My heart jolts from a combination of nerves and excitement as I dig for my yarn-bombing supplies. I'm so glad I convinced my brother to do this. We haven't spent time together in way too long. Lately it seems like Adam is only interested in doing stuff on his own, rather than with me.

Adam's the one who told me yarn bombing — which is street art for knitters and crocheters — existed in the first place. He helped me do smaller, lesser yarn bombs in our neighborhood the past couple of years. Mostly we covered parking meters in colorful knit cozies I made. We'd wrap a wool cuff around each pole, and Adam would hold it in place while I sewed the seam to keep the yarn bomb on. Once, we made a whole row of parking meters different colors — a rainbow instead of familiar gray.

But Adam says Ronny the Rattlesnake will be even better than that — he'll be our magnum opus. Adam says stuff like magnum opus.

I slip the sweater over Ronny's head. It's gold and brown, my school colors and the colors of Southern Pacific rattlesnakes, which Ronny is modeled after. The sweater alone took me two weeks of furious knitting to make — it even has a stripe with a diamond pattern down the back. I push and tug and push and tug until most of the snake's twisty length is covered in the wool tube. Then I wrap a thick brown scarf around Ronny's neck so he looks like he's either home with an epic sore throat or off to a stylish party.

But when I glance over at Adam, he's looking off in the distance. And not in a keeping-watch kind of way — more in a thinking-about-something-else kind of way, which is pretty weird.

"Hey," I whisper. "Yarn bomb in progress."

Adam shakes himself as though he'd fallen asleep and stands up really straight. "Sorry. Momentary lapse. But honestly, you're such a pro at this. You barely need me."

"Completely untrue," I say, my eyes practically cresting my forehead.

Adam smiles at me. "You can do anything, Zin. Remember that," he says before returning to guard duty.

I go back to winding the scarf around Ronny's neck. On the last twist, a car horn honks, and Adam and I both jump. I instinctively hide behind Ronny, and Adam drops the duffel bag to leap behind a shrub.

But no car pulls up, and nobody appears. Campus remains still.

Since the honk was a false alarm, I pop back out from behind Ronny. For a moment, I don't see any sign of Adam. That is, until he emerges from the foliage, pretending to walk up an imaginary staircase. He gets taller and taller, the shrub first at his shoulder, then his waist, then his knee.

"Hold on," he says. "I need to go downstairs for a second." Then he turns around to walk *down* an imaginary staircase too.

I laugh as quietly as I can. Watching Adam's pranks never gets old, but still — we have a yarn bomb to finish before the sun comes up.

"Want to put on the final touch?" I ask.

Adam bounds over the shrub and back to the statue. He reaches into his bag to retrieve the last part of Ronny's ensemble — a length of metallic gold fringe. With a flourish, he wraps it around the rattlesnake's tail, where it twinkles like tinsel. Then we stand back to admire the new Ronny, almost every inch of him now covered in yarn.

"What do you think?" I ask Adam.

"Fancy rattlesnake," he says. "More than fancy. Spectacular. Amazing." He balls up the duffel bag and tosses it in the air before catching it.

The sky is growing brighter now, our signal that it really is time to go.

"Farewell, Ronny the Amazing!" says Adam as the sun rises over our rattlesnake yarn bomb.

"Team Flossdrop forever," I say.

We spin in a circle, twirling and fist-pumping the air, the sky above us tangerine swirls.

Adam was right. This *is* the best ever. The very best.

2
YARN—BOMB FLOP

Adam was wrong.

Two hours later I'm back at school, and this time I am definitely *not* fist-pumping the air.

The rest of campus is happy and bubbling about summer vacation starting. There's even a table set up with brownies and cupcakes. I'm the only one not happy.

Ronny the Rattlesnake is naked — again.

Someone must've taken off his adornments. *Someone* must not understand knitting or public art and has probably never even heard of yarn bombing or anything else cool. I mean, yarn bombers secretly put an exuberant sweater on the whole world. That's what I wanted to do with Ronny.

Ugh. Nobody gets this stuff besides Adam. Nobody gets *me*.

"Zinnia Flossdrop," Ms. Amaranth, my vice principal, says as she approaches. "Just who I was looking for. You'll be spending the day in my office."

I close my shocked mouth and breathe through my nose. "What?" I can't comprehend what she's saying.

"Detention. Today. My office."

I'm confused. This is the last day of school. And I didn't even know you could get detention in the vice principal's office. I've only heard of the normal after-school-in-the-library kind, and I've never had that. Pretty sure my mom's bun would unravel if I did. Dr. Flossdrop is not the kind of person to approve of something that involves sitting around doing nothing.

"What do you mean?" I ask again.

"You're the one responsible for putting a costume on the school mascot," says Ms. Amaranth.

I want to tell her it isn't a *costume*, but that would be incriminating. "Why do you think *I* would do that?"

"Zinnia, I've been informed that you're a *knitter*." She says *knitter* like it's a bad word.

"Who told you that?"

"Someone I can trust."

No one comes to mind *I* can trust besides Adam. Operation Yarn Bomb was our secret, and he was my accomplice.

I follow the vice principal's gaze to the brownie and cupcake table. Next to it stand Nikki, Margot, and Lupita — my former friends. The four of us were once a pack. We used to roller-skate and have sleepovers and stay up late talking and laughing.

But that was months and months ago, at the beginning of seventh grade. And before that, in sixth. And before that, in fifth. We used to be Nikki, Margot, Lupita, Zinnia — NMLZ, like animals, for short. Nikki was the funniest and most outgoing, prone to random cartwheels. Margot was a dancer and super confident; she'd started wearing thin headbands this year, a few of them all at once. Lupita was the sweet one; her favorite color was purple, and she hiked every weekend with her family. I was the one known for wearing only charcoal gray and having massive, curly hair.

But something changed this year. Now they're NML. One animal. Without me. I'm a lone Z off on my own.

NML stare in my direction. Their faces wear smiles — fake, innocent ones. The smiles of ex-friends who can't be trusted. The smiles of people who spy on you and, when the time comes, spill it about all the stuff you thought you'd kept under wraps.

I can't smile back at them. I want to. I want to smile like I don't care at all that they've betrayed me. But I do care. And if I try to smile, my eyes might betray *me* and cry.

I take one last look at Ronny over my shoulder. Poor Ronny the Rattlesnake without so much as a pair of underwear, much less a fabulous yarn-bomb outfit.

I know exactly how he feels — exposed.

Ten minutes later, while the other kids are outside devouring baked goods, I'm in the vice principal's office.

The administrative assistant is eating a cupcake with chocolate frosting and yellow sprinkles — school/rattlesnake colors — at his desk. He hands me a pencil and paper and tells me to write an essay about what I plan to do on my summer vacation. Then he goes back to eating his cupcake. Slowly. Frosting with sprinkles first.

I figure since I've already been betrayed as a knitter, I might as well work on my never-ending scarf. That's better than writing an essay no one will ever read.

Sitting down, I open my backpack to retrieve my scarf and the wooden knitting needles attached to it. It's my never-ending scarf because, well, it never ends. I've continued knitting it long after it became an appropriate length for a scarf. Every time I get to the end of a skein of yarn, instead of binding it off and being done, I join on yet another skein in a different color. I'm on bright red right now. At this point the scarf barely fits in my backpack and would probably be better suited for a fashionable giraffe than a human. But I don't want to stop.

I knit and knit, getting lost in all the loops. The administrative assistant doesn't say anything about my lack of writing — maybe because he feels bad for me.

With each knit, each purl, each loop, each stitch, detention and NML and all that stuff gets further and further away. That's why I can't stop knitting. It's so much better when all that other stuff disappears.

I daydream about what I'll do this summer instead of writing it down. I want it to be exactly the same as last summer. Me and Adam again. The way it should be.

That's part of why this morning's yarn bomb was so great — it was a way for us to hang out, like we always used to. Just like we will this summer. We'll eat ice cream at Scoops together. Watch French movies at Aunt Mildred's. Do the five-dollar-bill trick at Dr. Flossdrop's office.

Adam and I did that trick a million times last summer. It involves taping a five-dollar bill to some clear fishing line, putting it in the middle of the empty waiting room, and waiting for someone to walk in and reach for the money. That's when Adam yanks it away.

When that someone realizes they've been tricked, Adam always does this ridiculous over-the-top bow — he waves one arm around all silly, twirling his hand and gesturing, and sticks one leg out in front of him. It's his signature. Admittedly it's pretty weird, but that bow makes people laugh every time instead of being mad.

I sit in detention, knitting and purling and daydreaming. I can't wait to see Adam to tell him all about this whole horrible yarn-bomb flop. He's the only one who'll understand.

3
MESSAGE

When I'm finally released from the vice principal's office, the day's June gloom has lifted; it's hazy and hot on my walk home after a miserable last day of seventh grade. At least I can look forward to commiserating with Adam about the injustice of it all.

But first there's a message from my mom. A sticky note with the words FROM THE OFFICE OF PHILOMENA FLOSSDROP, D.D.S. greets me on the door when I get to our side of the duplex.

The sticky note is the most common form of communication my mother and I have. She leaves them on the front door for me all the time. Almost our entire relationship fits on these tiny sheets of paper that could easily blow away in the wind.

Today's note informs me that my school called to report the *mascot incident* and that we'll discuss my punishment later. Of course Dr. Flossdrop wants to talk about punishment without knowing I've already been punished. Betrayed. Detained, etcetera, etcetera. She's probably going to want to *give* me a cavity for this.

I *whoosh* open the door to the duplex. It's dark inside, despite the heat of the day. Down the hallway, Adam's door is open, which means he's probably not in there. He doesn't leave his door open when he's in his room anymore. Not since he started turning into more and more of a loner, always carrying his secret notebook and keeping me out of the loop.

Wait a minute. Down the hall, *my* door is closed. And a pair of boots sits outside it. Blue work boots.

Dad's boots.

Those boots are part of a story I've heard my whole life.

Dad was a carpenter, but he had to stop working right after he built my crib because he got sick. Once I was born, he had to stop doing pretty much everything. When he wasn't in the hospital, which wasn't often, he could only lie in bed. But those boots were still his prized possession. When Dad died, he left Adam his boots as a way of saying goodbye and also as a way to remember him.

I was just a baby, so I don't remember anything about my dad on my own, but Adam was six. He remembers. Thanks to him, I've known about those blue boots forever. And I know Adam loves them more than practically anything. As soon as he turned sixteen a couple years ago, they fit him perfectly. He wears them almost every day. He was just wearing them this morning.

But Adam's not wearing them now. They're sitting right here outside my door.

Then it hits me.

The boots are a message, just like Dr. Flossdrop's sticky note. Except this message is heavy. So heavy it could never blow away in the wind.

It says goodbye.

And you only say goodbye when you're about to be gone.

The skin on my arms and legs bristles with cold, and I run into Adam's room. Some of his clothes are missing from his closet. His bike is still in here, which is pretty weird considering he basically rides it everywhere. Despite driving big trucks at Starving Artists Movers, where he works, Adam doesn't ever drive a car.

In a frenzy now, I search the duplex for a note to tell me where he is and when he's coming back and why in the world he left without saying goodbye in person.

I don't find anything.

Maybe Adam didn't leave. Maybe he put his boots at my door for another reason. Maybe he left the boots for me to shine them. Or to yarn bomb them. Or as a way of telling me we're going to have exactly the same summer I daydreamed about during detention.

But none of that makes any sense.

Dad said goodbye with those boots twelve years ago. And now Adam has said goodbye to me.

But where could he have gone? And why? And why in the world would he not tell me he was going?

Dr. Flossdrop won't let me have a cell phone, so I use the phone in the kitchen and call Adam's number. It rings and rings. When it finally goes to voicemail, it's not his old message. His old message was him talking like a robot, saying, "Adam Flossdrop, human on planet Earth, looks forward to communicating with you. Beeeeeeeep. Beep-beep-beep." And then the phone would actually beep.

Now all I hear is an automated message saying this number is no longer in use.

I check the number and try again. Same automated message. So either Adam has been kidnapped or he's canceled his phone service or changed his number. And I don't think he's been kidnapped if he left me goodbye boots.

I fling open the door to my room. Then I grab the boots and hurl them under my bed as hard as I can, like I never want to see them again. But that doesn't feel right. These are Dad's boots that Adam loves. And even if this is the meanest thing Adam has ever done — which it is — at least he tried to leave me something of himself, something to hang on to, the way Dad did for him.

But Dad's goodbye was permanent, and Adam's can't be. Adam's coming back. Adam *has* to come back.

I duck down and stand them up straight instead, their blue spines neatly in line. Then I collapse on my bed, unzip my backpack, and cuddle my never-ending scarf. I count the squares on my bedspread, hoping for the soothing effect counting always has on me. I get to 24 before giving up. It's useless to think about anything but my brother.

Adam was the magician at my ninth birthday party. When I turned ten, he made me a giant cardboard hat. When I turned eleven, he took me to an art museum and made me wear a sandwich board that said it was my birthday. When I turned twelve, he planned a scavenger hunt, and I had to solve clues to find out where we were going. It ended at the fountain downtown, which we swam in until security kicked us out.

Adam told me once that he was named Adam and I was named Zinnia because our dad wanted his kids to experience everything in the world from *A* to *Z*. That's how I used to feel with Adam, like we had all the letters of the alphabet connecting us.

But now he's left me here, a dangling *Z*.

I'll turn thirteen next year. Will Adam even be here?

I take all my confusion and sadness and shape it into something else. Something stronger, with sharper edges. I point it at Dr. Flossdrop, fast and fiery and full of thorns.

She's the one who drove Adam away. All their conversations this past year have been variations on the same theme: Dr. Flossdrop wanting Adam to go to college and medical school and Adam not wanting to.

It's all her fault. Adam would've stayed with us forever if Dr. Flossdrop hadn't pushed him to be more like her, if she'd just let him be a performer or a magician or something — himself. The true artist he is. She's the reason he's been getting distant, and now he's gone.

Even my never-ending scarf feels scratchy rather than soft when I remember how their fights had gotten worse and worse lately. Dr. Flossdrop was always warning Adam not to be *useless*. Uselessness is Dr. Flossdrop's archenemy, right after sugar. She's probably the most useful person on the planet. If someone finds a lost cat, she'll find it a home. If there's a pothole, she'll report it. If you have a petition, she'll sign it.

That's what she thought Adam was doing — acting useless. Working at Starving Artists Movers and doing the five-dollar-bill trick and hanging out with me would never qualify as useful to her. I remember the sound of yelling. The sound of the front door slamming on Adam's way out of the duplex. The small sound of yarn and wood in my damp hands once the house was silent again.

My mom may not have literally pushed Adam out the door, but she might as well have.

I make a vow. I'll look for Adam even if he doesn't want to be found. Even if he let me down in the worst possible way. Because he is Adam, and I need him, and that's the only thing I can do.

4
NEIGHBORHOOD ACTION

The closer I get to Dr. Flossdrop's office, the harder it is to breathe. Suddenly the warm air feels so gritty and stale, I don't want to take a breath at all. I usually love summer, even with my immense, curly hair weighing me down and my charcoal-gray clothes soaking up the heat, but right now rain and fog would be a better match for my mood.

Dr. Flossdrop and Adam and I have lived in a duplex down the street from her dental office my whole life. This lets my mom walk to work. That's convenient, especially because she's always there, even after regular hours when she sees patients who can't afford to pay. Her philosophy is summed up in the poster that hangs in her waiting room: HEALTH CARE IS FOR PEOPLE, NOT PROFIT.

I guess I can't disagree with that, even though there are no posters with mottoes about children or family in her office or our home.

The closeness of Dr. Flossdrop's office to the duplex is also convenient because she's perpetually holding neighborhood action meetings there on topics like raising money for the library, fixing potholes, and holding pet adoptions. Useful stuff like that.

I wish Dr. Flossdrop was more like Aunt Mildred. Honestly, it's hard to believe they're sisters considering how opposite they are.

Dr. Flossdrop lectures me about brushing and flossing; Mildred brushes my wild, tangly hair away from my forehead in order to kiss it.

Dr. Flossdrop doesn't watch TV or even own one; Mildred hosts movie screenings for Adam and me.

Dr. Flossdrop always wears her hair in a high, neat bun. Whether it's six in the morning or nine at night, I've *only* ever seen her hair in that bun. Mildred changes her hair every few months — she even dyed it pink once.

Dr. Flossdrop has a tiny, angular frame. She's as slim and metallic as a robot made of steel. And she doesn't allow sweets in our home, no exceptions. She would outlaw them from the world if she had the power. Mildred, on the other hand, bakes and advocates for oatmeal cookies. Her hips are spongy and wide. Despite that, she has the most miniscule fingers, able to nimbly scrape the hardest-to-reach back molars.

That's right, Aunt Mildred is Dr. Flossdrop's dental assistant.

Up ahead I spot the white building. Then the sign: DR. PHILOMENA FLOSSDROP, D.D.S.

I want to see chaos. Police officers, big LOST SON signs like the ones Dr. Flossdrop prints when pets go missing.

But when I walk inside everything is the same. Pink carpet. Pink walls. Pink sofas. (Mildred did the decorating.) The large sign that proclaims HEALTH CARE IS

FOR PEOPLE, NOT PROFIT. Brochures for various causes. Classical music piped in. Pink saloon doors leading past the reception desk to the exam rooms — to Dr. Flossdrop herself.

The waiting room is fairly full. Even with the music playing I hear Mildred somewhere in the back. I follow her voice. She's humming a French song about the ocean. When I find her, she's got on scrubs with rainbow polka dots all over them. She immediately wraps her arms around me in one of those hugs that I'm sure makes us look kind of like the spirally layers of a cinnamon roll. I smell *her* cinnamony scent. Even when she's not baking in her kitchen, that's what Aunt Mildred smells like. Even here in Dr. Flossdrop's sterile office.

I melt, but only a little. I'm on a mission to find out about Adam.

"Bonjour, mon pous," says Mildred.

"Adam is gone," I tell her.

"My poor cat," she says, tussling my curly hair around with her tiny hands. "I'm sorry."

"Where is he?"

"Oh, macaroon, I haven't a clue."

Just then, Dr. Flossdrop approaches. She's dressed in her usual all-black outfit with a white lab coat and black clogs. Her hair is in its tightest, highest bun. Her left hand is clenched in a fist, which is pretty weird.

I glare at her, trying to muster the courage to yell and scream and throw patient files in the air so they can rain down around the three of us. But instead, I stand there. Silent.

Dr. Flossdrop proceeds to say three things:

1. "We'll talk tonight about what happened at school."
2. "I'll be home late."
3. "Please put these flyers in the waiting room on your way out."

There's a stack of flyers in her right hand. As soon as I take it, that hand also clenches into a fist. She looks like she's getting ready for some kind of fight, but she's a pacifist so that's impossible.

She says nothing about Adam.

I stare at her like she is a robot and not a person.

And then she's marching back down the hall in her clogs again, fists clenched.

"Mom," I call after her.

But she doesn't hear me. Or she does, but it doesn't matter. She doesn't turn around.

"Ugh," I say to Mildred, who rubs my back in wide circles. I turn to her. "You knew Adam was gone?"

Mildred nods. "There was an ace of hearts on my welcome mat this morning. I knew there was no one else it could be from. Then I talked to your mom, and we figured it out."

"Wait. So she knows?"

"As she put it, she 'saw this coming.' He left her an envelope with rent for the past three months."

"But she didn't say anything about him just now!"

"Honeydew, your mom's pretty worked up."

"Worked up?" I look at Mildred the way any self-respecting twelve-year-old looks at an adult when they're talking nonsense. "She doesn't *seem* too worked up."

"On the inside she is," says Mildred.

"Yeah, right," I mutter. "The only thing she cares about is the *inside* of people's mouths."

Mildred's quiet for a second. "What about potholes?" she asks with a smile.

I can't help but smile a little too. "Yeah, she does care a lot about potholes. Potholes and vacant lots and anything else she can fix in the neighborhood." I pause. "So he really didn't tell you where he went?" I ask quietly.

Mildred shakes her head and gives me a sad face. A really sad face. Like she understands. But no sad face could be sad enough to mimic how I feel. My sadness is a giant, gaping, betrayed sadness beyond description.

"One thing I do know," says Mildred, "is that Adam wouldn't have left without a good reason. That boy has something he needs to do."

I growl. I can't be mad at her because she's Mildred, and I know she's trying to cheer me up, but the thing is, I can't imagine one single good reason why Adam would've left. Especially without telling me first. There is no possible reason for this deception. It's the kind of thing Dr. Flossdrop is normally signing Internet petitions about, but when her own son does it, she says nothing.

"I have to get to work, so you'd better yank outta here like a rotten tooth," says Mildred.

I give her a hug goodbye and head out, dropping Mom's stack of flyers on a side table in the waiting room on my way. Then I make the mistake of reading one. It's a petition.

NEIGHBORHOOD ACTION ALERT

TREE-PLANTING PETITION

The meadow has no trees. Let's plant some!!!

Name	Email	Phone Number

The exclamation points at the end are what really get me. Dr. Flossdrop never uses exclamation points unless she's talking about a neighborhood action project. She definitely never uses exclamation points that way about me.

I want to dump those tree petition flyers in the trash. But then I remember I should recycle them, and the recycling bin is back in the office. I settle for turning the stack upside down before I leave.

I know exactly where to go next. It's one of Adam's favorite hangouts and the only place I can think of that he might be. He used to play ukulele there sometimes and put out a hat for tips. Plus, the place I'm thinking of is also Dr. Flossdrop's arch nemesis . . . right behind uselessness, that is.

It sells ice cream.

Bees
WE ARE THE BEES

We are a colony. We are, by definition, a group.

We — worker females, drone males, the queen — operate collectively. One for all, and all for one.

Most of the time anyway.

The story we're about to tell you is about a colony of honeybees. Our colony. Our story.

We were commercial, migratory bees. In other words, we were not out there on our own, free. We were rentals. We were tended by beekeepers who employed us to pollinate food for humans. Food like apples, pears, almonds, cherries, cucumbers, cabbages, blueberries, celery, papaya, pumpkins, and for certain humans, Brussels sprouts.

We were jet-setters. Well, truck-sitters. We traveled across the country to all kinds of places to carry out our industrial duties of pollinating flowers so the trees and shrubs of the field would produce fruit.

It wasn't a bad job once we were at an orchard, and the getting of pollen and nectar was good. But the tang of pesticide in our proboscises and the long days of rumbling highways in between were exhausting. Not to mention the sickeningly sweet syrup they fed us on the truck to tide us over until the next stop. And let's not get started on pollen patties. They are not an adequate substitute for the real thing.

But we were workers for hire who did our jobs buzzingly. The beekeepers were kind to us; we had no gripes with them. But still, deep inside our exoskeletons, we were unhappy. We felt trapped — literally.

We wondered if there might be another way.

We were on that truck a lot of the time, squashed between other wooden box hives. So we spent those long rides scheming ways to get out. We wanted to find a place to settle down in nature the way our ancestors would've done. Not the ancestors who traveled across the Atlantic in 1622 in the straw hives of English colonists to become the first Americans of their kind, but the many who came after them. The ones who roamed free and found wild places to nest and go about their honey-making, queen-protecting business.

We'd heard rumors of other bees who'd managed to escape. In fact, some of the hives that pollinated with us at orchards had recently up and disappeared. Just like that.

The problem was, we had no idea where they'd disappeared to. Or if they'd survived.

Despite the risk of great danger, there came a point when we decided, together, that we'd had enough. Better to risk failure than to never try. There was only one thing to do.

Make a break for it at our very first chance. And hope, with each and every one of us crossing all six hairy legs, that we'd get one.

5
OPERATION ICE CREAM

Customers are scattered at metal tables outside Scoops. Seven tables and Adam is not at any of them. He's not at any of the five tables inside either. And he's not one of the four people in line for ice cream.

I wait to see if he'll come out of the bathroom, which is locked, but when the door opens it's a woman with a crying baby. Not Adam.

I really hoped that he would be here. That he'd explain everything. That he'd just forgotten to leave me a note. But instead, my second place to scout for Adam is a total failure too.

I decide to console myself with ice cream and take revenge on Dr. Flossdrop at the same time. My mother may not believe in sweets, but one of Aunt Mildred's mottoes is, "Everyone deserves dessert." (That includes people who teach dental hygiene for a living too.) And I definitely deserve dessert today.

I order a cone of mint chocolate chip served in a cup — the best of both worlds — and take it outside. I choose a table far away from the others. Even though a scoop at Scoops is always amazing, right now it looks and tastes like slime. I set my cup down; I don't feel like eating after all.

Soon the ice cream gets melty, which is my favorite, but I still can't bring myself to take another bite. It trickles from the tip of the cone, down and over the cup, across the shiny silver tabletop. The cone finally topples over, and ice cream spills everywhere. I watch as my frozen treat morphs into a sad green stream, then slowly drips off the table onto the ground.

Drip.

Adam is not here.

Drip.

Adam is gone.

Drip.

Adam taught me how to swim. How to sneak sweets behind Dr. Flossdrop's back. Mildred taught me to knit, but Adam taught me how to yarn bomb.

For every time I haven't had a dad around — or a mom, for that matter — Adam's been there. For as long as I can remember.

My body feels like a sandbag. I lay my heavy head on the table and hope no one worries that I've collapsed from ice-cream poisoning. That's when I start crying. The table rocks, the cone rolls, and ice cream dribbles into my hair. I can feel its coldness drizzle through tendrils the same way I can feel tears drizzle down my face. I don't care, though. I don't wipe my face or my hair. I don't move. I could stay hunched over this table forever, drenched in salty tears and mint-green glop.

I'm there for five long, miserable minutes. Then a loud crash from the street jolts me back. It reminds me I can't really stay slung over this table forever.

As soon as I get up, I see a few adult-types looking at me with concern. Then I see the thing responsible for that loud crash. Right there on Sunrise Boulevard, a big truck loaded with wooden boxes has skidded onto the sidewalk and collided with a nearby streetlight. The driver's out of the truck and seems to be OK, but there's smoke and a crowd of people are gathering to see what happened.

I feel bad thinking it, but at least someone else is having a horrible day besides me.

I stand up, and ice cream dribbles from my hair onto my collar, turning my charcoal gray T-shirt slightly wet and minty green. I throw out the ice cream cone and cup, leaving the drippy goop all over the table, and silently ask Dr. Flossdrop and anyone who works at Scoops for forgiveness for not cleaning up.

Heading in the general direction of home, I pass the sneaker store and art supply store, but the smoke from the accident gets my attention. Some of it is definitely smoke, poofing up and dissipating into the air. But some of it's moving more like a cloud — a rippling, blurry cloud. It looks like a cloud of bees. A cloud of bees rising up from one of the boxes on the truck.

I stand there, staring, wondering what bees are doing in a box on a truck in the first place. Then I feel a small gust of air as something flies past my face. It's a bee. I don't know if it's a regular bee or an escapee from the smoky truck, but either way, I'm out of here. I'm not allergic to or super afraid of bees, but the fact is, they're no one's favorite animal for a reason.

I shake out my ice-creamy hair and keep going. There are plenty of people around to help with that accident. Adult people. And I am definitely *not* my come-to-the-rescue mom.

But as I glance back, there's that bee again. It's making its way toward me like it's delirious — mostly going in a straight line but veering around a little too, like maybe the wind is blowing it. Lollygagging the way bees do. But still, lollygagging in my direction.

I keep walking — faster now — but when I glance back again, just to see what's going on, that bee is closer behind me. Or maybe it's a different bee. They all look the same.

Wait a minute.

All of a sudden it's not just *one* bee anymore. It's a few bees. Then a handful. Then a whole bunch. Before I know it, it's a whole swarm of bees! My eyeballs are overwhelmed with too many bees to even count. What *was* an undulating gray cloud over the truck is now an undulating gray cloud above the sidewalk — and it's headed straight for me.

I walk as fast as I possibly can — trying not to bring attention to myself — but the bees speed up too.

This. Is. Pretty. Weird.

As I hurry down the street, I think of stingers and welts. I could really use one of those full-body suits with a mask. Because that clump of bees is most definitely on the move.

Suddenly one bee breaks away from the others and zips toward me. It circles a foot or two away. It darts toward me for a second, then goes back to circling again. Then it darts closer. This time it keeps coming, a slow-motion swoop in my direction. All I can do is stop right where I am and helplessly shield my face, hoping the bee will abandon whatever mission it's on.

For a moment, I feel nothing. I peek between my face-shielding hands and see nothing.

But then there's a tingle on the crown of my head.

Not a sting, just a tingle.

I wave my hand around. Nothing happens.

And then there's another bee aiming straight for me.

Nonononono!

I shield my face again, but like its predecessor, this bee isn't going for my face. It's not going past me either. Instead, I feel a second arrival in my wild, curly, ice-creamy mop of hair. Another tiny little weight.

More bees are coming toward me now. They're close enough that I can see the way their spindly little legs dangle below them as they fly. Their papery, translucent wings. The soft sound of an old-timey phone ringing.

Bbrriinnnnnnngg. Bbrriinnnnnnngg.

I take off down the sidewalk in a panic, tripping over people and shoes and strollers. It's like a terrible, ridiculous attack-of-the-bees sci-fi movie is being filmed — except no one else knows about it, and I am, unfortunately, the star.

People turn and look at me, but my legs and mind are moving too fast to care or hear them if they're trying to talk to me.

I keep running. I don't look back.

I run for blocks and blocks. Past sneakers hanging from telephone wires. Past kids on skateboards. Past the lady who sweeps up trash. Past the neon-bandana bike-riding guy. Past a food truck.

I'm getting closer to the duplex.

And then I do look back. Just to check.

There's no use running anymore. The whole swarm is circling, closer, closer, closer. A remote-controlled airplane engine in my ear. Hundreds of bees uncomfortably near my bonnet.

And then they're landing.

All of them.

On my head!

Bees

GETAWAY

Finally the chance came.

We felt ourselves tumbling this way and that, our wood hive cracking and splintering. If we wanted to be, we were free.

We looked from fuzzy face to fuzzy face and nodded, terrified but sure. We zoomed away from the broken boxes and the truck. All four thousand of us, the heart chambers of our abdomens thrumming.

The best temporary landing pad was a telephone wire on the street. Shaking from shock and woozy from exertion, we quickly composed ourselves and festooned. We hooked our tiny toes together and created a U-shape from one part of the wire to another, clinging to each other for dear life. We must've looked not unlike a long, thick, wiggly beard. It must've been a very fine-looking beard.

But we weren't finished. We had to act fast. We immediately elected a scout — a female worker bee who could go out and search for a suitable new home. We desperately needed a new one now that ours had been shattered and abandoned. But we had no idea where to find a hive or even what it should be. All we could see around us were buildings and streets and people and signs. No more almond orchards.

We chose Bee 641 to be the scout.

Bee 641 had never done any home-finding before, but of course none of the rest of us had either. We'd all been born and raised by benevolent beekeepers who gave us premade wood homes.

But everyone believed mightily in the choice. Because we had to.

Bee 641 stuck out her antennae, legs dangling limply beneath her, all four of her wings alighting from our bee beard. *The shops and traffic signs glistened in the thousands of black lenses of her eyes.*

She wandered, hoping to find the hollow of a tree, but she had no such good fortune. For our colony of bees, home meant either a box on a truck or the hollow of a tree. That's all we'd ever known — the first from experience, and the second from stories the queen told at bedtime.

Our family — all four thousand of us — was depending on Bee 641.

So off she flew. When she smelled something sweet, she followed. She saw a glint of green on top of a nestlike mass.

Maybe those are leaves, she thought, *a kind of leaves I've not seen before. Leaves and twigs and silt. It's not a tree, and it appears to be moving, but it's something.*

OK, it was a stretch. But these were stretching times.

Bee 641 immediately returned to the telephone wire. Our colony took no time querying about the location of the new digs. We unlinked our toes, giving them a kick to unfurl, and we were off.

Bee 641 led the way, and we followed.

There, there! *she signaled to our gang behind her.*

We flew toward what resembled a shrub atop a torso and legs. We landed, one by one, and quickly configured into the shape of a proper hive. The opposite of a long, thick, wiggly beard. More like a high, wiggly clump.

But as soon as we'd caught our little breaths and assessed our surroundings, we set about accusing Bee 641 of being completely and utterly unreliable.

Leaves? Twigs? *we raged.* We beg to differ.

Poor Bee 641's mandible quivered.

How do you expect us to live here? Where will we put the honeycomb? The young? How will we survive?

But we already had our answer. We were stuck. Again. This time on top of a human's head with copious amounts of hair thinly coated with sugar.

We may have been naive — OK, we were naive — but we truly thought we had nowhere else to go and no other options. We looked around, considering our situation. All we could do was shake our heads at Bee 641.

6
WORST EVER

I grab a free newspaper from a stack on the street. I open and drape it over my head to hide the fact that my hair is a buzzing, swarming mass of bees.

I keep moving toward the duplex, trying to distract myself with other things, one hand on my newspaper hat at all times.

Blue mailbox. Bees.

Big truck. Bees.

Billboard. Bees.

Black hat. *Bees, bees, bees!*

Finally, I spot the oleander hedge on the sidewalk, and beyond it Dr. Flossdrop's yard of drought-tolerant plants. Lou, who lives next door to us in the other half of the duplex, is using the pull-up bar in his door frame. Wiry gray hairs peek out of his V-neck T-shirt, which is wet with sweat. He's squinting from the effort of his pull-up.

Lou is an ergonomic coach. I've seen countless clients slump up the steps and into his hallway only to march their way back down. The sign on Lou's door, which is only visible when it's actually closed because he's not using the pull-up bar, reads ERGONOMICALLY CORRECT.

But now is not the time to watch Lou do a pull-up. I take advantage of his squint by slithering up the steps to the front stoop, hoping he won't see me or my newspaper hat or the bees underneath it.

"Hey, Zinny! How are ya?"

I stop. Lou sees me.

"Fine, Lou," I reply, hoping the conversation will end there.

His eyes are fully open now, even though his feet are still off the ground, the rest of him suspended in midair. His biceps are twitching, but he keeps talking to me.

"How many times do we have to go over this, kiddo? Call me Coach." Lou winks and laughs, and in doing so, lets his elbows release. His athletic-shoed feet fall to his welcome mat.

"OK, Lou. I mean — sorry."

"You sure you're fine?" he asks. "Because you've got an *Eastside Weekly* on your head, and it's not raining. It is solid sun protection, though."

"Yup! All fine here. Have a good workout!"

Whoosh!

I'm through the door before Lou can say anything else. I run to the bathroom, wishing desperately that Adam were here so he could tell me if this is really happening. I'm sure he'd know just what to do. He'd have some idea that would be part performance art, part solution. Adam can do anything.

But Adam's not here.

I shut my eyes in front of the bathroom mirror and release the newspaper down to my side. I stand there like I'm at a sleepover back in the day when Nikki, Margot, Lupita, and I used to play those Bloody Mary games way back when we were still NMLZ. I spin around slowly three times and prepare for what I may or may not see when I pop open my eyes.

There I am reflected in the mirror.

My hair looks like it's in an old-timey beehive hairdo. Except this hairdo is a real beehive composed of real, live bees that are constantly moving and shifting and scurrying.

I can't see my hair at all except for the slight dip of the widow's peak on my forehead and the curly strands that hang below my ears. Everything else is a moving, itchy, disgusting, insectian mess.

I open the bathroom window and stand next to it, hoping the fresh air will convince the bees to flee.

Nothing happens.

I flutter my hands around above me.

Still nothing.

I shake my head in a way that hurts my brain. I dance around. I scream.

Nothing, nothing, nothing.

I try to coax a bee onto a Q-tip, the way you would if you were rescuing one from a pool or something.

It will not be coaxed.

I thought my summer was doomed with Adam's departure, but now this . . . *this* is truly the worst ever.

I picture growing old with a zillion bees as my only companions. Knitting alone, rocking-chair shoulders hunched from my helmet of creepy crawly creatures, their small dental drill drone buzzing in my ears.

It's not a soothing image.

Since I don't think bees can swim, I decide to take a bath and count the tiles on the ceiling. There's nothing else I can do but wait and see what happens next.

7
MEET MILKSHAKE

The *whoosh* of the front door brings me out of my daze in the now cool, soapy bathwater. Someone is home. It's either Adam or Dr. Flossdrop, and I hope against hope for the first.

I close my eyes, submerging all but my mouth and nose underwater, wishing this whole long, terrible day was a dream. But when I resurface, it's not a dream. The bees hover in a cloud over me, but they refuse to fly out the still-open bathroom window.

I gradually lift my head from the water, hoping they'll stay in their formation near the ceiling. But as soon as I'm upright they come back to roost on the roots of my wet hair.

This is beyond pretty weird. It's a plague. And apparently it's *my* plague, so I'm going to have to figure out how to keep it a secret without wearing an *Eastside Weekly* everywhere.

I grab a towel to dry off and decide my hoodie — charcoal gray, just like everything else I own — will work. I put the hood up to hide the bees. It's a little like wearing socks when you have sand all over your feet — only it's wiggly sand.

When I emerge from the bathroom, Dr. Flossdrop is crouched on the hardwood floor. Next to her is something small, furry, and slightly wet.

My mother looks up at me briefly and then back at the creature. "What are you wearing that hood for?" she asks.

I can't contain myself. "You got a *dog*?" I demand. When her son disappears, Dr. Flossdrop adopts an animal. The very same day. It's like she really can't be alone with me.

"He's a terrier," she replies. "But let's talk about what happened at school."

"What about Adam?"

"What about dressing up the school mascot in a demeaning outfit?"

"It wasn't a demeaning outfit. It was a yarn bomb."

"A yarn *bomb*? That sounds violent."

"It's not. You just unravel it. Nobody gets hurt. Not even Ronny."

"Who's Ronny?" asks Dr. Flossdrop.

I ignore her question. "What if Adam is in trouble? Or a runaway?" I ask.

"Adam is eighteen years old. He had a full-time job at that Starving Artists place and paid rent. He can't be a runaway," she says. "And the only trouble he's in is with me."

Yeah, I think, even though she's the one who drove him away with her constant Starving-Artist nagging, urging him to do something useful with his life.

Dr. Flossdrop takes a dog treat from her purse. It looks super disgusting. The trembling, sweating, wheezing dog gathers the strength to gnaw it.

"Your punishment for the yarn-bomb incident is to walk Milkshake once a day while I'm at work."

"Milkshake?" I repeat. And I thought water was the only Dr. Flossdrop-approved beverage.

"That was already his name. He's from animal services. He seems to have asthma, and nobody wanted him. He might've been *killed*." Dr. Flossdrop stares at me, laser-beaming guilt into my eyes. "Now, like I said, you'll need to walk him once a day. You can retrieve him at the office."

"You're taking a dog to your office?"

"It's not the first time I've sheltered a pet there."

I barely resist the urge to roll my eyes. For someone so concerned with oral hygiene, you'd think Dr. Flossdrop would be a little more hesitant about bringing a stringy, damp dog to work. I just hope she washes her hands before putting them in people's mouths after petting it the way she is right now. Because it's *gross*.

"That dog is too small to even be considered a dog," I say. She has no idea how many creatures have entered my life today — all of them small and annoying.

"He's a perfect dog. Aren't you the perfect dog?" It's then that my mother's voice turns into something I've never heard before. It's gooey and caramelly and all the things she never cooks or eats or acts like. It's sweet as sugar. She even makes baby-gurgle noises at the dog before moving in for a repulsive, horrifically slobbery kiss.

I'd rather see myself in the mirror with bees on my head again than be watching this, but somehow I can't look away.

"Milkshake and I are going to sleep. Good night," says Dr. Flossdrop, ignoring the fact that we're in the middle of a conversation. She does look tired, but also kind of happy. Some tendrils of hair have escaped from her usually impeccable bun, probably from petting the dog, and this gives her face a softness Dr. Flossdrop doesn't normally possess.

Yup, she looks sort of *happy* with this dog named Milkshake.

And that is just too much for a brotherless person with bees on her head to handle.

8
MEET BIRCH

The Internet isn't any help. I look up *Adam Flossdrop* to see if he has any social media accounts I don't know about or has been mentioned somewhere, but I find nothing. Not that I was really expecting to. My brother isn't a big computer guy and has never been into posting stuff online — he's old-fashioned that way. But the past few months, Adam hung out at the meadow a lot with his newly *secret* notebook, so I'm going to look there for him next, in real life.

The meadow is this big expanse of grass on one end of our neighborhood, some of it pretty tall and meadowlike. Our duplex is on the opposite side of Sunrise Boulevard, basically halfway between the meadow and Scoops. Anyway, lots of people go to the meadow to read or fly kites or hang out on blankets in the sun. Some people are doing those things right now. And luckily, with my hood on, no one seems to notice that I'm secretly Bee Girl. The perfect disguise.

But *unluckily*, none of the people at the meadow right now are Adam. So much for my plan.

I remember when we used to come here together every summer. We'd lie on our backs watching the sky. Doing nothing. It was like the ultimate rebellion in uselessness. One time, Adam showed me how to whistle with a blade of grass. He plucked one, lined it up between his thumbs, and blew, his cheeks puffed.

"That sounds like a kazoo," I said. "Or a goose."

"Yeah, a goose in a lot of pain," said Adam. It took a few tries, then he did it again. "That one sounded like a fart."

"That's gross," I said.

"But it's true."

"Yeah, it's kinda true." I paused. "Do you think Dr. Flossdrop has ever farted?" I asked.

"Yes, but I've never heard it. Or smelled it. A Dr. Flossdrop fart is like a rare mushroom that only thrives in very particular conditions, too rare for most humans to sense or smell."

I plucked my own blade of grass and put it between my thumbs. Pulled it taut. Puffed my cheeks and exhaled.

Nothing happened. Adam told me to cup my hands more.

Finally, it worked. My whistle was higher pitched than his.

"Yours sounds like Aunt Mildred on helium. *Bonjooooooouuuuuuuur!*"

I whistled. Adam whistled. We whistled at the same time in a hilarious clash of sounds like party horns. People looked at us, but we were laughing so hard we didn't care. We were our own little meadow orchestra. We were everything.

But now I'm all alone. Except for you-know-what on my head. And with no idea how to make *them* go away.

Last night, I stayed up knitting in bed as long as I possibly could. When I eventually got so tired that I had no choice but to lay my head on the pillow, I did so carefully, thinking only of being stung on the delicate ridges of my ears. But the bees didn't sting me. They also didn't leave, even to hover like when I was in the bath. It took me hours to relax, especially since I didn't want to toss or turn.

In the morning, they were still there — despite me having left my bedroom window open as an invitation for exit. I didn't have to look to know. I could not only hear them, but feel them, sense them, like fingernails grown out too long. Impossible to ignore, but something you can live with. Sort of. If you absolutely have to.

Now, in the meadow, I climb up a small hill by the fence at the perimeter. I take this hidden moment to retrieve one of the extra knitting needles I always keep in my back pocket, remove my hood, and scratch my scalp for ten seconds of relief. But when I replace the hood, my head is immediately a hot, itchy hive once again.

Way out in the middle of the meadow I spot a tall, lanky boy with binoculars held up to his face. He's acting very strange. He keeps pointing those binoculars in what seems like my direction. Then straight up in the air, then straight back to me again. The boy's neck cranes up, then over, then down toward *me* every time.

Binocular guy appears to be coming closer. I try to act natural and ignore him, but there's nowhere for me to go what with the fence behind me. I'd like for the grass to magically grow even taller and encompass me completely. I mean, he *looks* twelve years old, but maybe he's an undercover operative here to investigate my bee situation. Anything could happen at this point.

Agent Binoculars get closer and closer. The rest of him looks normal, if a little plaid — plaid red-and-blue shirt, faintly plaid tan-and-red shorts — but his face looks like a giant mutated fly on account of the binoculars.

But then he takes them from his eyes and places them around his neck. He's now only two feet away, and without binoculars, I can see his eyes. They're kind of greenish-silver and remind me immediately of the ocean.

This tall, plaid-wearing boy is looking at me like he's on a field trip to a natural history museum, and I'm a stuffed woolly mammoth. Something you can ogle and maybe even touch and it won't care because it's stuffed.

I adjust and secure my hood. I don't appreciate being stared at, and I definitely don't appreciate how he's reaching out his hand to possibly pet me.

I jump and yell, "Who are you?"

"I'm Birch," the boy says.

For a moment, I freeze in place. But then I realize I need to get away from this guy. I shimmy a little to the side, inching elsewhere.

Birch takes a small step in the same direction I moved.

I step.

He steps.

I step.

He steps.

Then we both step in sync until we're circling each other, boxers in a ring.

Finally, I have to put a stop to this. "Stop!" I shout. "What are you doing?"

Birch suddenly seems to realize that the answer to my question is that he's been staring at me, but he doesn't say that of course. "Bird-watching," he replies.

"Bird-watching?"

"Yeah."

"I don't see too many birds."

"Well, that's the problem, actually. Once in a while one flies overhead — I've seen a hawk, two crows, and a few mourning doves — but I have to spot it midflight, and all that spotting is making me dizzy. There are no trees in this park for larger birds to rest or nest in. Actually, there are hardly any trees in this whole neighborhood."

Of course I take this as an insult and a challenge. "There are too trees here."

"Really? Great! Where are they?" Birch's eyes get really big. They have faint circles around them from the binoculars.

While I want to defend my neighborhood, the truth is I can't think of anyplace — within walking distance anyway — that has a whole bunch of trees. Maybe that's why Dr. Flossdrop wants to plant them here at the meadow.

"There's a skinny tree out front where I live," I finally say.

"Cool," says Birch. "Me too."

"And there are some along the sidewalk down there." I point across Sunrise Boulevard, in the direction of Dr. Flossdrop's office and the duplex.

"What kind of trees?"

"The tree kind," I say.

Birch nods like that was an actual answer.

"Where are you *from*?" I ask.

"You've never heard of it."

"Try me," I insist.

"It's a little town up north."

"Well, *Birch*, is it called Oak?"

"Ha. Close! Redwood City."

"You're joking," I say.

"Nope. So who are *you*?"

I begin counting the plaid squares on his shirt.

"What are you doing?" I hear Birch asking me.

"Nothing. Zinnia. My name is Zinnia." Here we are, a flower and a tree.

Birch grins. "Well, *Zinnia*, are you from *Rose*mont? Bell*flower*??"

"No. I'm from here."

"Cool."

Birch doesn't protest anything I say. It's as if, in addition to his eyes, his mind is also like the ocean. It's wide and open, and you can throw whatever you want into it, and it will swallow it up without resistance. Which I find pretty weird.

"OK, bye!" I start to walk away, across the meadow and toward the street, but Birch follows. And keeps talking.

"There are actually a lot of trees in Redwood City," he says. "And there's water too. Birds love water, especially egrets and cormorants. That's why I bird-watch. There are tons of birds there. And we have the best weather in the world, actually. There was a scientific test, and we tied as the best-weather winner with two other places in the whole world. That was a long time ago, but I think it's still accurate."

I walk a little faster, approaching the crosswalk. Birch with his long, tall legs keeps up.

"Who *made* you?" I ask him.

"My parents, I guess. Actually, they're naturalists."

"Wait a minute. They go around naked?"

Birch stops following me. He stands back there, laughing the binoculars around his neck into a shake. "No. They're into nature. Science, trees, rocks. Stuff like that." He's still talking pretty loudly even though he's caught up to me again.

"Lemme guess. Birds?"

"Yes, my parents like birds too," he says.

Finally, the pedestrian light turns green and I take off, making sure my pace doesn't mess with the placement of my hood. Birch crosses the street too.

"Um, can I ask you a question?" he asks.

I don't answer. I get to the other side of Sunrise Boulevard, one hand on the knitting needle in my back pocket like it's a sword I could use to defend myself with if necessary.

Birch asks anyway. "How did you get those bees to stay on your head?"

I stop and gape at him. Maybe he has X-ray vision and can see through my hood. I mean, the lines in his green-silver irises are kind of lit up, which may be a sign.

I try unsuccessfully to play it off. "What bees?"

"Ummm . . . how do I put this?" Birch scrunches his face, looks off in the distance, and then back at me, pointing his finger vigorously toward my hooded head. "Maybe you don't know this, but there are, well, honeybees, I think. On top of your head. Or in your hair, I guess?"

I'm stunned. I can't even move. Only the bees under my hood stir, their constant scurrying aggravating whiz. "Birch, that's absurd."

I take off again, this time practically running.

"You can't even see my head!" I yell behind me, clutching my hood to keep it from inching down.

I can hear Birch's footsteps behind me.

"I can't see them right now, of course," he says. "But I did, back in the meadow. I think they're about the coolest thing I've ever seen."

I make a wish for Birch to stop talking and wander off somewhere to contemplate his naturalist discovery.

But of course he doesn't.

"And, actually, I've seen a lot of cool things. The giant sequoias, for example. A webcam of a baby eaglets' nest. And one time, at the beach, a seal who'd washed up on shore was getting rescued. That was really cool. But not as cool as this."

Birch has seen my bees, but there's no way I can trust a stranger enough to admit he's right. How can I trust anyone ever again after NML betrayed me? After Adam cleared out without a word? No thanks.

"Are you following me home?" I ask the bird-watching, me-watching spy over my shoulder.

"No. I've decided to call it a morning myself. My uncle's probably ready for lunch. When I arrived last night he promised we could have junk food because my parents never let me have any. My uncle says they eat like squirrels. He wants me to try eating like a human during my visit. Or maybe like a bear. He kind of reminds me of a bear, actually."

Birch continues to trail me.

Right beside the duplex's oleander hedge, I crouch down like I'm going to retie my shoelaces. I hope he'll proceed without me.

Nope. Birch stops too.

"What are you doing?" he asks.

"Nothing."

"It doesn't look like nothing." He stands there and waits for me to finish pretend retying my laces.

I stand back up and gesture to the duplex. "Well, this is my place. Bye, Birch!"

"Actually, this is my place too."

The two of us simultaneously step past the hedge, but at that, I stop short.

"What? Wait a minute. What's your uncle's name?"

"Lou. I'm staying with him this summer because my parents think he's lonely. I'm here to keep him company."

I stare at him. "I can't believe this. You're my neighbor."

9
BRAIN FREEZE

"Hey, Birch! Zinny! Looks like you kids met!" There's Lou, doing pull-ups in his door frame, able to shout even though he's probably on pull-up number three hundred or something.

"Zinny, wanna join Birch and me for lunch?"

As much as I usually pretend polite indifference to Lou, because he winks and uses words like *snazzy* and is old but fit in his athletic pants, I secretly like him. I even secretly like that he asks me to call him Coach, which I have never once done. I don't go around calling people Coach.

But while I like Lou, I'm not so sure about the invitation. Especially since Birch might let the bees out of the hood.

"There will be ice cream," Lou adds.

Since my side of the duplex offers leftover tofu-cucumber salad and cereal and that's about it, I can't bring myself to turn down his offer.

"If you put it that way, OK," I say.

The three of us enter Lou's duplex single file, passing the CHALLENGE poster in Lou's hallway that has a picture of a woman climbing up the side of a steep rock face. Lou loves motivational posters. There's a quote underneath the rock climber that really sticks out to me today:

"NOTHING EXTERNAL TO YOU HAS ANY POWER OVER YOU."
— RALPH WALDO EMERSON

I'd like to talk to this Ralph about what's arrived on my head to see if he might change his mind about that.

Lunch is very small sandwiches and very large bowls of ice cream. I opt for chocolate chip on its own, while Lou and Birch dunk Ding Dongs into their portions to make them even more junk-foody.

Once the bowl is before me, I can't help but think back to yesterday and wonder whether there's a connection between what's in the bowl and what's on my head. After all, the bees arrived after I went to Scoops. Maybe ice cream makes insects act wacky. For all I know, dragonflies will soon appear in Lou's kitchen and attach themselves to my fingers like opulent rings. I guess it's a risk I'm willing to take, though — having bees on my head is bad enough without having ice cream off-limits.

I take one bite and then another.

Lou's television's blaring on the kitchen counter, so we're all pretty quiet as we eat. Some show with a lot of arguing is on. I can't even tell what they're arguing about, it's so loud. Lou never looks at the screen, but he refuses to turn it off or down.

He does, however, tell me that my sweatshirt hood may be affecting my alignment and points out that I'm hunched over my ice cream bowl. He suggests I should take my hood off — and offers me free ergonomic coaching. I decline both.

Birch has somehow, amazingly, never tasted ice cream before. This guy is pretty weird. Dr. Flossdrop would probably love this fact about Birch except that on his first taste, he describes it, through shivering cheeks, as "delectable." Then he digs in again and again and proceeds to get his first brain freeze. I know because he slaps palm to forehead in the universal language of brain freezes.

"Put your tongue on the roof of your mouth," I tell him through my own mouthful of creamy vanilla and crunchy chocolate chips.

Birch obeys, and Lou and I wait a few seconds for him to remove his palm from his face.

"Ouch. I owe you," Birch says.

"No you don't. I have a lot of experience with ice cream," I say.

"What does your mom have to say about that?" Lou asks.

I ignore his question, instead focusing on counting the number of chocolate chips left in my bowl. Eleven.

"Earth to Zinny," says Lou.

"Oh. Um. Let's make ice cream our little secret, OK?" I say.

"Safe with me," says Lou, confirming that despite the gray tufts of hair spilling from his V-neck shirt, he is still the best grownup I know — right after Mildred, that is.

"What, does your mom only eat squirrel food too?" asks Birch.

"Kind of. But it's more about sweets. She's a dentist."

"No way."

"Yes way."

"That's the coolest thing I've ever heard."

"I thought the bees were the coolest thing you've ever —" I quickly zip my mouth closed. Maybe *I'm* the one I should worry about spilling the beans. Or bees, as the case may be.

"What bees?" asks Lou as he gets up from the table to stretch.

"Coolest thing I ever *heard*. Not *saw*," Birch corrects, ignoring Lou's question.

"Well, dentists aren't really that cool," I say. "Trust me."

"I disagree. Dentists are scientists — your mom probably knows all kinds of stuff."

"Hey, folks!" Lou asks again, shouting to be heard over the screaming television, me and Birch talking, and the water he's started running in the sink. *"What bees?"*

We still ignore him.

"Dentists don't know any stuff better than how to cure brain freeze," I tell Birch.

"OK. Maybe not better than that, but —"

Lou turns to us from the sink. "Are bees some kind of code for drugs? Come on, you can tell me."

I frantically look at Birch, telepathically telling him not to mention the bees. *My* bees. *Please, please, please.*

Thankfully, Birch catches on.

"No, Uncle Lou! I saw a nature documentary, and it showed how bees actually dance! It's called a waggle dance, and one of them does it to lead the others to something important. Their little bee butts wiggle around. It's really cool."

I'm relieved to learn Birch can think on his feet. Now I just want to get out of here to avoid any more close calls.

"Oh. That is pretty cool. Way better than drugs, kids. Believe me."

Lou starts doing his own bee waggle dance while he washes dishes, swishing his athletic-pant behind in the most ridiculous way.

I'm about to slink from the kitchen, but Lou starts talking again.

"You know who can really dance? Adam."

At that, I no longer want to slink away. I want to hear what waggle-dancing Lou is saying about my brother.

"He borrowed boxing gloves from me a couple of weeks ago, and that kid can move!"

"Boxing gloves?" I repeat, perplexed. Adam who never exercises and has never been in a fight? Now I'm the one who feels like I have brain freeze.

"Yeah. I guess it's not technically borrowing since he mentioned he was going to paint them some outrageous color, but that's Adam, right? Gotta love that kid."

"Who's Adam?" asks Birch.

"Nobody," I say.

Adam isn't nobody, of course, but he's beginning to feel more and more like a stranger.

Lou starts singing his own original waggle song while he continues doing dishes and dancing. I finally leave the room. Birch follows — of course.

"Thanks for making up that stuff about waggle dancing," I say as I head for the front door.

"Actually, I didn't make it up," says Birch.

"Oh. Well, thanks for making up that that's what we were talking about. Bees on TV. Not that there are any other bees on the premises," I add.

"No problem. Now we're even for the brain-freeze remedy."

"Sure," I say, practically flying out the door. "Please tell Lou thanks for lunch!"

"OK," says Birch, but he seems like he wants to say something more. He's fiddling with the cuff of his plaid shirt when I look back at him from my side of the duplex.

"Hey, Zinnia, do you want to try Lou's . . ."

I don't wait to hear the rest of what he's going to ask. Instead, I grab the sticky note Dr. Flossdrop has left for me, reminding me to go to her office and walk Milkshake and that there's tofu-cucumber salad in the fridge, and close the door.

Whoosh.

I already know what Birch wants to ask. He's probably dying to talk about the bees. And while he may have kept my bees a secret from Lou, I'd rather not continue Birch's scientific inquiry. No one is to be trusted at this point. I mean, look at Adam and those boxing gloves. I'm starting to think I don't know my brother at all. I'm starting to think that nothing is reliable. Everything feels new and unpredictable and out of whack.

Talk about brain freeze.

Bees
SPAKE THE QUEEN

Life in the makeshift human hive might've been considered a step up from our life as truck-traveling hired pollinators. But make no mistake, we were not oozing gratitude.

First, we were weary, practically starving, having already scoured any remaining pollen remnants from our legs and sucked each other's proboscises dry of every last drop of nectar. That sugary film on the human's head didn't last a minute, not that it hit the spot anyway. We even went so far as to try eating the layer of oil beneath our living quarters, but it tasted horrible.

Worse than being tired and hungry, we knew our big chance had failed. Possibly our only chance.

We looked around and didn't see many trees or reliable food sources. We were used to being cared for by beekeepers, our lives a semi-predictable routine. And now, here we were, on our own. We had no idea what to do.

We longed for a real home. To build honeycomb in a place of our own. To seal the cracks with bee glue. To guard our nest. To do chores. To raise young. To work hard and see the fruits of our labor.

We longed for the extended waggle dance of a forager telling of wild delights to be found in the distance. We even longed for the sudden intrusion of a bear's massive claw into our honey-dripping hive. Those were things we'd heard of, tales passed down from colony to colony for generations. That's what we thought we were escaping to. But those were things only dreamed of for now.

Mostly, we grumbled.

There was grumbling about the noise, the lack of noise, the light, the lack of light, the temperature, the food — the lack thereof — and every other facet of our accommodations.

And there was continuous grumbling about a certain inexperienced scout who clearly should not have been trusted.

Yes, we spent most of our time complaining loudly and pointing our collective antennae at Bee 641, pleading to the queen for some kind of justice.

Bee 641 spent most of her *time curled up in a ball, legs wrapped around her thorax.*

Until the human moves somewhere with hibiscus flowers and pomegranate trees, we are stuck with her. We shall stop being petty and make the most of it. And that is that, *spake the queen.*

And that, indeed, was that.

10
THIS IS MY LIFE NOW

A milkshake is a drink for special occasions, like to celebrate winning a game or getting a good grade. You might buy a milkshake for a person who's feeling down. I associate Milkshake the dog with no special occasions or good times. I associate Milkshake with dribbling urine on the floor of the duplex, even though I take him on a walk to go to the bathroom once a day and Dr. Flossdrop walks him to and from work too. He only does this in my or Adam's room, of course.

Dr. Flossdrop, however, maintains that Milkshake has excellent bladder control because she can find nothing wrong with him. Shocking, considering that he's Adam's replacement, and she found a lot wrong with Adam.

I am in the minority regarding my opinion of Milkshake. People love stopping us on our walks in order to pet him. They might be pretending, but they act like they think he's really sweet. Maybe some people are genuinely fond of wheezy, sweaty dogs.

One such person is currently petting Milkshake and thus preventing me from getting home and knitting the bees out of my head if not away from it. I'm looking around, trying to find an escape route, when I spot Nikki, Margot, and Lupita. Right there on the sidewalk between Dr. Flossdrop's office and the duplex. Coming my way.

"We have to go," I tell Milkshake's admirer, whose face falls into a disappointed slouch. I don't care. All I care about is avoiding NML.

I steer Milkshake down the street and toward the oleander hedge, which I proceed to hide behind, crouched down to Milkshake's height. Even though the leaves are pointy and known to be poisonous when eaten, I stick my face through so I can see NML.

Lupita wears purple, like always. Margot has a bunch of skinny headbands on, some braided, some flat. NML are laughing together, and right at this very moment Nikki is throwing her head back like she's having the greatest time of her life.

I wonder what they're talking about right now. I mean, don't they remember that this is where *I* live? Where we used to have sleepovers after roller-skating? Do they ever even think of me? Maybe only when they want to betray me.

I lean farther into the oleander hedge in order to keep spying, so much so that I'm teetering on my tiptoes. That's when Milkshake, with more gusto than I've yet to see him display, decides to take off. He tugs on the leash, which slips from my hand and makes me tumble.

I fly out from behind the hedge, onto the sidewalk.

Right in front of NML.

They stop abruptly and look down at me, all three of them, wondering at this spectacle before them. At least they stop laughing.

Milkshake sniffs their shoes.

Before they have a chance to say anything, I scramble to my feet in the most ungraceful way possible, awkwardly adjusting my hood placement. I really don't need them to see the creatures I'm hanging out with these days. But I feel compelled to say something. Something to hurt them like they hurt me with their betrayal.

"Thanks a lot for turning me in on the last day of school." Then I grab Milkshake's leash and rush back from whence I came.

"Zinnia?" I hear Nikki and Lupita say simultaneously.

But I'm not about to turn back. I get to the door of the duplex as quickly as I can while still avoiding being stuck by one of Dr. Flossdrop's cactuses. I'm frozen there as NML continue walking by the hedge, murmuring something to themselves that I can't hear.

When they're gone, I swivel my head to find Birch standing at Lou's door. He looks like he's preparing to do a pull-up. He's probably been preparing to do a pull-up this whole time. But now, acting like he didn't just witness that whole humiliating scene, he stares at the bar above him, taking deep breaths, and shaking his arms that dangle out of his plaid sleeves.

We make eye contact, and Birch strains to pulls his body up off the ground. He only manages to get his eyebrows level with the bar before having to let go. Apparently, he's a lot taller than he is strong.

I open the door to the duplex — *whoosh* — and let Milkshake inside. I try to slide in after him to avoid more humiliation, but Birch interrupts.

"Hey, Zinnia! Who were those girls?"

"Nobody."

"They didn't seem like nobody."

"We used to be friends."

"Used to? What happened?" asks Birch, who apparently never tires of inquiry.

"They betrayed me."

As I say it out loud, I realize I don't know *why* they betrayed me. I mean, sure, we'd been drifting apart all school year until we might as well have been living on different continents. It was like the opposite of magnets — we were pulled *away* from each other by some invisible force.

But I don't know *why* they told the vice principal about Ronny. Yeah, they started snubbing me and leaving me out. They looked at me funny when I knitted my never-ending scarf, and they spent all their time texting each other. They didn't want to hear about Adam or yarn bombing. Eventually they no longer invited me to roller-skate — or whatever it was they were doing now. But they'd never done anything overtly mean to me before that. That's the kind of thing I'd remember.

"Whoa. Betrayed you? That's sounds bad," says Birch. "But hey, do you want to try Lou's — "

Birch is asking me something. But I'm not listening. I'm already through the door.

11
GOODY

Wood needles. Wool yarn. The hypnotizing push and pull, tuck and wrap. All the stuff that feels massive gets smaller. Less overwhelming. It fades into faraway stars. Dots that don't concern me.

Just the movement of my fingers, the click of needles, the tug of string.

It's not far from the best ever.

Until the front door opens — *whoosh*.

I put down my never-ending scarf. Everything comes at me again. Massive and close and gaining ground.

Dr. Flossdrop. The *calunk* of her clogs.

NML.

The bees.

I've tried leaving the windows open all week. I've tried shaking my head furiously. I've tried taking hour-long showers, despite what Dr. Flossdrop thinks of wasting that much water. I've tried asking them politely. I've tried yelling, too.

But the bees aren't listening. And they're not leaving.

Unlike Adam, who left and might never be coming back. I haven't heard from him, and I haven't seen him, even though I'm always looking.

Everything feels impossible again. Big and fast and suffocating.

"Zinnia!"

I return my hood to its upright position as quickly as I can, just in time for Dr. Flossdrop to pop her head around the corner of my bedroom door. The soggy bagpipe that is Milkshake plods along beside her.

"Zinnia. I wanted to ask you something." Dr. Flossdrop appears to still think nothing is amiss with her daughter, so I doubt the question will be about my insect infestation.

"Is it about Adam?" I ask.

Her bun appears to tighten at the mention of his name, which she ignores. "It's about what you're doing this summer. What are your plans?"

I resume my knitting. "I don't know. Walking Milkshake. Nothing."

Milkshake chooses that moment to flop down on Dr. Flossdrop's black clogs. He proceeds to slobber on their soles.

"You can't do nothing. It's not an accurate answer. You're doing something now."

"OK. I'm doing this."

"Yarn bombing?" Dr. Flossdrop gestures to my alarm clock, which I've yarn bombed so that three sides of it now feature black-and-yellow knit stripes to match what's always on my head *and* regularly on my mind. Then she looks at the legs of my bed, two of which are wrapped in orange yarn. The two she can't see are wrapped in neon pink.

"Am I not *allowed* to yarn bomb?"

"If you're not defacing public property, I guess it's fine."

Fingers. Needles. Yarn.

She tries again. "So you'll be knitting then?"

Now we both look at my never-ending scarf, draped over my dresser and down one bedpost and across the floor. I'm working with electric blue right now. I'm going to use this same color to yarn bomb my headboard later. I'm basically planning on making my bedroom a comfortable knit chamber since I might spend the rest of my life in here without human company.

I don't answer.

"I just wondered if you had a plan."

I kind of have a plan. But it involves looking for Adam, and one thing I know for sure is I *won't* be telling Dr. Flossdrop that. She's acting like Adam never existed at all. I stay silent.

"Well, then, I have a way you can make yourself *useful* this summer," my mother says, walking all the way into the room. She carries a canvas bag, which reminds me of Santa's sack, and proceeds to empty it onto my bed. Without asking. Then she gestures to the mountain of stuff — toothbrushes, little cartons of floss, and plastic bags with pictures of a smiling anthropomorphic tooth on them. It's like a sick toy shop for dentists has erupted on my comforter.

Dr. Flossdrop explains that I will put stickers that say PHILOMENA FLOSSDROP, D.D.S. with the office's contact information on everything. Then I will put one of each item into the plastic bags with a smiling tooth. They'll be goody bags for patients. The kind of thing most parents give out at birthday parties when you're little, except those are filled with candy.

I never had goody bags at my birthday parties. Well, technically I had them once, but they were filled with persimmons, which were in season. After that I asked Dr. Flossdrop to stop with the goody bags.

For some reason, I can't help but think of NML and their parents. Of the kind of input they have into their daughters' summers. Like maybe they take them on vacation. Or send them to camp. Or eat dinner with them.

I remember the stuff Margot carried in her backpack for her dance classes when we were still friends and NMLZ — slippers and a tutu for ballet, sneakers for hip-hop. Nikki's family road trips to a big reunion every

August. Lupita goes camping on the beach with hers the last week of every summer.

Thinking about NML makes my face flush as I remember my embarrassing run-in on the sidewalk. Maybe they'll all move away together this summer so I never have to see them again.

"Oh, and these, too," Dr. Flossdrop says. She takes out a stack of what look like business cards from her purse. One side says HEALTH CARE IS FOR PEOPLE, NOT PROFIT, just like her poster. The other says ZT4BG in big letters.

"What's ZT4BG?" I ask.

"Zero tolerance for bleeding gums! Have I taught you nothing?"

I'm still considering how to answer this question when Dr. Flossdrop exits my room, leaving behind the mountain of goody-bag ingredients, Adam's miniature wheezing replacement following along behind her.

12
UPSIDE DOWN

I'm assembling my fourteenth goody bag in seven hours when there's a knock at the door. Admittedly, I've only assembled fourteen bags on my first day of this *useful* task because I had to sticker everything first — then I took a long break to work on my headboard yarn bomb. Then I yarn bombed one of Dr. Flossdrop's coffee mugs with part of a scarf I had lying around. Not that she'll ever notice.

I also took a break to think about where in the world Adam might be. I even searched through Dr. Flossdrop's encyclopedias in desperation to see if Adam had dog-eared any pages or left a slip of paper between them, like a clue of some kind. He hadn't.

There's another knock — small but persistent. It could be a mail carrier or someone from an organization asking for a donation. We're kind of a hot spot for donation-seekers thanks to Dr. Flossdrop's endless neighborhood action activities. I don't want to answer. Even with my hood up, I feel like Zinnia, the lonely bee-laden oddball. All I want to do is hide.

But it doesn't sound like whoever is out there is going away. I creep to the front door and peek out. The knock's tall, skinny, plaid owner stands there. Waiting patiently. Clearly not going anywhere.

I open the door — *whoosh*.

"Hi, Zinnia. How are you?"

Birch holds out a FROM THE OFFICE OF PHILOMENA FLOSSDROP, D.D.S. sticky note that must've been waiting for me on the outside of the door. On it, Dr. Flossdrop asks me to take out the trash. I guess that's my other big, useful plan for the summer.

"I'm fantastic," I say. I can see Birch looking at my eyes, then above my eyes, at my forehead and the place where my hood juts out over my hair. "What do you need?"

Birch refocuses on my eyes. "Nothing. Actually, I wondered if you'd like to try out Uncle Lou's inversion table."

I don't know what that is, but I know better than to ask. "No, thanks."

"Oh. OK. Well, maybe another time?"

"Maybe."

"It's pretty cool. You flip upside down, and it feels strange . . . but in a good way. It also takes pressure off your spine and helps with your alignment in case there's anything bothering yours. You know, like . . ." Birch gestures with his plaid shoulder toward my face, and his eyes get even bigger.

"OK, fine. I'll try it," I say. I figure I could throw him this little thing he seems so set on. Let's face it, all I have to do right now is stuff goody bags and take out the trash for Dr. Flossdrop.

I follow Birch down my steps and over to Lou's. We pass Lou in the front yard, busy working with an ergonomic client. They walk barefoot in slow motion next to one another, trying to put each toe down separately — pinky toe first — as they do. It's pretty weird.

Birch and I pass the pull-up bar and rock climber CHALLENGE poster, then head into Lou's equipment room. I hear the TV booming from the kitchen, even though nobody's in there.

Birch points to a metal and plastic contraption. "Here it is," he says.

The inversion table looks vaguely like a torture device. Staring at it, I wonder if it's still possible that this is just a ploy to make my hood come off so Birch can inspect the bees with his naturalist eyes. Perhaps with his binoculars.

I consider bolting, but don't.

Birch eases me onto the table, which is kind of like a folding lounge chair that doesn't fold, and I stand awkwardly upright. He fumbles a little while securing my feet with a strap, and I pull my hood forward, pressing the back of my head against the table so it stays put.

"Ready?" asks Birch.

I give him a half smile.

Birch tips the whole contraption, and I tip backward until I'm suspended upside down. Blood rushes to my head like fire. But at least I can feel sweatshirt fabric lodged behind me, and the front lip of my hood still grazes my eyebrows. Bees, covered and secure.

After a few more moments upside down, I completely stop worrying about hiding the bees from Birch. About the bees themselves. About anything at all. My brain goes cool. I'm weightless, like an astronaut or something. It's like when I'm in the flow of knitting. It's almost better than that.

The inversion table-torture device is possibly my new best ever.

I stare forward at another one of Lou's posters on the wall. This one — upside down at the moment — says LIBERATION, which is an appropriate view to have from this miracle table.

Above LIBERATION, there's a black-and-gray-and-white drawing by M. C. Escher that I swear was in my math textbook last year. It's shaped like a long scroll with wavy gray triangles at the bottom. The triangles get wavier and wavier higher up the drawing, some white, some black. Eventually two corners of every triangle distort into wings. The third corners turn into beaks. They keep shifting until the triangles change into birdlike shapes, eventually turning into actual realistic birds at the highest part of the scroll.

Since I'm seeing it upside down, it works in reverse — birds morphing into triangles. It works either way, though. Birch must like this print since it has birds on it. Pretty weird, but I like it too.

Somewhere in the background I hear Birch going on and on about what Lou said about the benefits of the inversion table.

Blahblahblah. I'm not listening to anything except the rush of gravity in my ears.

But just as quickly as this inversion table felt good, it starts to feel bad — bad like I might throw up. And right then, as if he knows this, Birch tips the table until I'm standing upright again.

I slowly come to out of my daze. Unfortunately, Birch is asking me something.

"So, can I see your bees?"

I knew it. This was just a trick all along.

"Ugh, there are no bees, Birch. I have to go." I unstrap my own feet and step away from the table.

"Come on, I saw them. You took your hood down at the meadow and scratched your head with one of those knitting needles you always carry. And you've basically admitted it."

"I do not carry knitting needles with me," I say in protest.

Birch leans down and picks up one of my knitting needles from the floor, where it must've fallen during my inversion session. He holds it out to me.

"Fine," I say, snatching it from his hand. "I do carry an extra pair of knitting needles at all times. And I do have bees on my head. But they're a secret. You're not allowed to *see* them or acknowledge them or talk about them."

"But then how can I help?" he asks.

"Help?"

"Well, I think they're awesome, but you don't seem to think so. And they're probably not awesome long term. Maybe I could help figure out how to get rid of them. Without hurting *them* of course."

I stare at Birch.

"Or hurting you," he adds. "Obviously."

"You want to *help*?"

"Of course! I mean, I'm curious too — in the name of science. But I promise I won't laugh or tell anyone or anything like that. Never."

The knitting needle I'm clutching is covered in sweat. I tuck it back into my pocket and take a long look at Birch. It's pretty weird, but I believe him. Besides, it's not like I have anyone else to talk to about this since Adam's gone. For sure not Dr. Flossdrop. Not even Aunt Mildred. She might be Mildred, but she's still an adult and would probably feel obligated to tell Dr. Flossdrop. At least Birch seems worth a shot. One shot. For one minute.

Before I can stop myself I bring my hand to my head and sweep the hood off so it falls down on my neck. I keep my fingers poised so I can bring it up again at any moment if I need to.

Birch leans in, still keeping a respectable distance. His lips part slightly in what looks like astonishment. He slowly walks in a circle around me and says a very small "Wow" from time to time. I feel like a woolly mammoth again.

When Birch comes to a stop in front of me, he tears his eyes away from my hair and focuses on my face. "Wow," he says again.

I put my hood back on and it's over. It was awful, but not nearly as bad as I thought it would be.

"I can't figure out why the bees would make their hive in your hair like that."

"Thanks for the help," I say with a huff. I start to make my way out of the room.

"Hey," says Birch. "I can't figure it out yet, but I'll work on it."

"And you'll help me figure out how to get rid of them?" I ask.

"I'll try," he says. "Don't worry, Zinnia. Your secrets are safe with me. Ice cream, bees. Mum's the word."

While I'm not familiar with that phrase, I get the idea. I also have this funny feeling he means it. Birch, who lets everything in so easily, will be good at keeping this thing in. My secret has been thrown overboard, which is terrifying, but it feels good to know it's been thrown into what seems to be a deep, wide sea.

Bees
STILL THERE

We were still there. Even though we didn't know where
there was. Most of the time we were covered by gray fabric, so
we didn't even have anything to look at. Not that there could
be much of a view when you're used to apple orchards and
strawberry fields. We'd been on our way to alfalfa and clo-
ver when the truck crashed. Alfalfa and clover! Those things
were unimaginable in our current, wretched existence.

The perpetual state of forced dieting, not to mention the
slight atrophy of our folded-up tongues and tucked wings,
was getting to us. Some of us even gingerly admitted that our

beeswax glands were backed up. We were still hungry. Still disgruntled. Worse, we were bored. Even the drones, known for their idleness, were antsy for something to pass the time.

Alas, the queen was glimpsed drumming her nails on an attendant's behind. Given the conditions, she'd stopped laying eggs. She was used to laying more than a thousand a day! She had even ceased production of her perfume, that sublime scent that signaled all was well with the hive. For all was not well.

We wanted a proper kind of beehood, our species' calling for millions of years — to work for our own well-being and the world's. To pollinate and produce honey. To thrive. And yet there we were.

So we came up with an idea. We formed Action Committees to brainstorm possible plans for obtaining a new home. But they were quickly nicknamed (Distr)action Committees. No one could concentrate given the circumstances. We talked about anything — mostly food and the yearned-for feeling of flying at fifteen miles an hour — other than the matter at tarsus of finding a home.

We renamed them Solution Summits, but it was more of the same. We were bees, revered for our ability to work together, for our productivity. But all of that evaporated with our newfound independence. Because we weren't independent. We were helpless.

Arguments broke out. Factions formed. There was even talk of revolt. Mutiny against the queen!

That was just the riffraff talking. No respectable bee would really dare such a thing, even without the queen's perfume wafting around to reassure us. Revolt was unthinkable. Downright despicable and un-apian. The queen and the colony were our universe. We'd be nothing without each other.

One faction spoke up and suggested trying to find the truck and the orchards, returning to life as agricultural automatons. If we could find a migratory bee truck, it would be more predictable. At the very least it would involve proper meals.

But that was perceived by the group as giving up. And bees don't give up so easily. It's simply not in our nature.

13
OPERATION STARVING ARTISTS

I open my front door — *whoosh* — and Birch is standing there, one hand in the air, preparing to knock.

"What are you doing?" I yell. "You scared me!"

"Oh, sorry," he says.

As if Birch could be any more predictable, not only is he at my front door — *again* — but he's also wearing plaid. Red-and-black plaid shirt, tan shorts, and socks that are checkered blue and green. It makes me glad I always wear charcoal gray — at least I'll never have to worry about clashing patterns with this guy.

"Where are you going?" he asks.

"Nowhere."

"Can I come?"

"Any progress on figuring out what to do about these?" I ask, gesturing to my hood.

Birch shakes his head. "Not yet."

"Then no," I say. His neck shrinks a little into his crumpled plaid collar when I say it, though, so I change my mind. "Fine, you can come if you promise not to ask any questions."

"You mean it's a secret mission?"

"Yeah."

"Cool," says Birch.

I've been working up the courage to visit Adam's workplace for days because, to be honest, this is kind of my last hope. And I've preferred to hang onto a little hope. Hope that my brother will return and, not only that, have the perfect solution to free me from the bees.

But even if he's not at Starving Artists Movers, maybe I can at least gather some intelligence as to his whereabouts.

Birch and I walk away from Sunrise Boulevard, down a side street and over the big hill where Mildred lives. We make our way to the other main road in the neighborhood, which leads to a more industrial area.

"Starving Artists Movers," says Birch when we arrive. "That's clever."

"OK," I say. "You're the lookout."

He salutes. "What exactly am I looking out for?"

"Anything that seems like a clue," I say, searching for a way to keep Birch busy — and in the dark about my brother — while I go inside the main office.

"A clue to what?"

"Anything," I repeat. But then I realize that if I'm really lucky and Adam *is* here, Birch's lookout position might be useful. "Also look for any eighteen-year-old humans. Please remember where they're headed if you see any."

Birch nods. "Got it."

"See you soon," I say.

Halfway to the office I slow, suddenly worried about just barging in there. About what I may or may not find. I pause and adjust my hood. I can feel the bees like a force field, their energy and movement and tiny wind. I look back, and Birch gives me a thumbs-up sign. His small gesture gives me the confidence to press on.

When I walk inside, the office is cramped and messy and smells like motor oil and plastic. There's a TV blaring in the corner. Some surfing reality show is playing. A man behind the counter glances up as I enter. He has a substantial beard and wears chunky metal rings on both thumbs, all of which makes him that much more intimidating to approach.

"What do you want, kid?"

I take his use of *kid* as a bad sign, but I answer anyway. "I'm looking for Adam."

He doesn't reply. Maybe he doesn't hear me.

"Adam Flossdrop. He works here," I try again.

"*Used* to work here. He quit. Never liked him anyway."

"Do you know where he went when he quit?"

The man taps one of his big rings on the counter in front of him. "Who knows with these artists? They're completely unreliable. They're late, they quit, their heads are in the clouds half the time."

Despite the name of the company, this guy really seems to dislike artists.

"So Adam didn't mention *anything* about his future plans then?"

"We weren't buddies; he was just one of the movers. Now run along, kid," he says, turning back to the TV.

That's that.

Conversation over.

When I return to Birch, he looks like he's about to burst. "I saw a human who looked about eighteen!" he whisper-shouts.

"Really? Where?" I don't imagine it's Adam given that the guy inside just told me he quit, but a tiny part of me flickers with hope.

Birch puts his finger to his lips and motions for me to follow him. We tiptoe around back to the truck lot and spot a middle-aged man with salt-and-pepper hair standing by a Dumpster, looking at his phone.

"Do you even know what an eighteen-year-old looks like?" I ask Birch.

"Not *him*," he says. "Our suspect probably went through that back door. Just wait. You'll see."

We stand next to a trash can on the sidewalk, in front of the truck lot, trying not to draw attention to ourselves. Sweat trickles down my forehead from the heat of wearing a hood and beehive in this weather.

"Hey, Zinnia . . ." says Birch while we wait.

"Uh-huh."

"Remember how I told you I'm here to keep Uncle Lou company this summer? Because he's lonely?"

"Uh-huh."

"Well, that's not the real reason I'm here," Birch confesses. "Ever since you trusted me with your secret, I've been meaning to tell you."

Oh no. I freeze. I don't need this right now. I don't need Birch revealing something, trying to bond, when I'm keeping something, everything, from him. I already showed him the bees. Isn't that enough?

"You're really here to study the flora and fauna of Southern California on behalf of Redwood City Middle School," I say as a distraction. "Look, there's one of those green flying beetles for your research right now!"

"Cool! But no . . ." Birch will not be swayed from this topic. He takes a big breath. "I'm trying to make the soccer team this fall because I haven't been able to before."

"What does that have to do with staying at Lou's?"

"My parents thought Lou could help."

"Wait a minute. Does Lou play soccer?" I ask. I've never seen Lou holding any soccer balls or wearing cleats or anything.

"No, Lou doesn't like team sports. But he's an ergonomic coach, so he helps with spinal alignment and fitness and all that."

"Your spinal alignment is why you haven't made the soccer team?"

"No. It's that, well, I'm really uncoordinated." Birch says this like it's a terrible, shameful thing to admit.

"Did your parents tell you that?"

"No," he says, shaking his head.

"The soccer coach said you were uncoordinated?"

"No one said it. No one had to. It's obvious. Watch this," he says.

Birch picks up a soda can lying near us on the ground and sets it upright. Then he takes a few steps back and dashes toward it. But when he attempts to kick it mid-dash, he trips. His shoe never makes contact. The can sits motionless on the sidewalk.

He turns to look at me. "See? I've tried out twice and haven't made the team. I want to play soccer, and I want to be part of things. My only real friends back home are in my bird-watching club, and they don't go to my school." He pauses before adding, "Actually, they're all adults. I don't really have any friends at school."

"Oh," I say.

The more Birch divulges about himself, the more I feel the uncomfortable prickliness of guilt. Adam and Mildred have been *my* only friends since NML excommunicated me, but I haven't told him that. I haven't even told him the reason for this whole mission or what we're doing here in this parking lot — who we're looking for.

"Soccer is my chance for things to be different at school this year."

"Good luck," I tell him. "I hope you make the team this time." I mean it. I really do.

I've been so busy with Birch's confession that I almost didn't notice an eighteen-year-old has emerged from the building. But even though I can only see the back of whoever it is, I can tell by the ponytail that it's not Adam.

The girl taps the guy with the salt-and-pepper hair on the shoulder, and he joins her at a moving truck. He rolls up the rear door, and the ponytailed-girl loads some big green quilts into the back. It looks like she cut her T-shirt with scissors all around the collar in some sad attempt to make that Starving Artists Movers shirt somewhat fashionable. One shoulder slips off while she's working, revealing a flock of gray-and-black birds tattooed on her skin — they fly up her neck and disappear behind her ear.

The girl finishes loading the moving pads, rolls down the door, and climbs in the truck. The guy gets in on the passenger side.

Feeling my opportunity slipping away, I head toward them. I try to calm my nerves by counting the letters in one of the words on the company logo. *Starving.* Eight. But before I can get close enough, the engine starts, and the truck pulls out of the lot.

I wave my arms around, hoping they'll see me in their rearview mirror, but they don't. Or they don't care. The truck turns down a side street and drives away.

"Sooo . . . what was that all about?" asks Birch.

"Nothing."

"Are you training to be an apprentice mover?"

"No."

"Do you think they're smuggling something illegal in those trucks?"

"No."

"Are you curious if any coyotes ever visit that Dumpster for food? Because I am."

I shake my head. "No."

I say it in a way I hope sounds final. It must because Birch stops asking questions.

We proceed down Sunrise Boulevard toward the duplex. I feel like crumbling — my disappointment adds to the already heavy burden of the bees — to the point that each step is a struggle. I think I finally have to admit to myself that I'm not going to magically find Adam in my neighborhood. That I probably won't find him at all.

Birch breaks the silence. "Thanks for listening earlier," he says. "I wanted to tell you about the soccer team as soon as I had a chance. I don't want to keep any secrets from someone who's my friend."

At the word *friend*, a mockingbird squawks loudly. Birch, ever the bird-watcher, looks up. I stare straight ahead.

Birch said we're friends and that friends don't keep secrets. But he must know that I'm keeping one right now. He must accept that I'm keeping stuff from him, the way he seems to accept everything. The way he accepts me.

But I'm not ready to talk about Adam. Not with anyone. Especially someone I practically just met. I keep my eyes straight ahead and don't respond. Somehow, without even saying a word, I feel as naked as Ronny the Rattlesnake.

14
OPEN DOOR

Mildred is outside Dr. Flossdrop's office helping a woman into her car when I arrive to deliver all the goody bags I've assembled. Once the car drives away, Mildred stands on the asphalt in the bright sun. Just the sight of her rainbow polka-dotted scrubs lifts my mood.

"Muffin Biscotti Zinnia!" Mildred never runs out of new ways to address me. "You might want to take that sweatshirt off and get some sunshine today, hon. It could do you some good." She looks worried as she pulls me into a twisty-cinnamon-roll hug.

I don't stay in the hug long; I don't want Mildred to sense the shift or buzz of bees.

"*A bientot,*" she says. "Off to save the world from gingivitis!"

Mildred takes the goody bags — 79 in total — and scuttles toward the office door.

"Oh, and go easy on your mother. She found out that even with so many signatures on her tree-planting petition, the city won't let her do a neighborhood action that big. I mean, who wouldn't want more trees? Trees are like nature's Eiffel Towers."

With that, Mildred disappears behind the door.

I'm left alone on Dr. Flossdrop's toothbrush welcome mat. But in the brief moment Mildred had the door to the office open, I saw three things:

1. A new poster on the wall next to HEALTH CARE IS FOR PEOPLE, NOT PROFIT. It's of a Yorkshire terrier, like Milkshake, only this one looks a lot more energetic.

2. Actual Milkshake, dozing on the pink carpet of the waiting room beneath the poster, wheezing.

3. A hand petting Milkshake's giant hairy ears — the hand of a boy with a plaid arm attached.

I open the door again.

Both Birch and the dog raise their heads, swinging around to look my direction.

"Zinnia!" Birch exclaims. Milkshake just lays his head down again and pants.

"Birch? What are you doing here?"

"Your mom told Uncle Lou I could have a free cleaning and exam. Dr. Flossdrop is an excellent dentist, by the way. Plus, no cavities! And look, Mildred just gave me this goody bag!" He lifts up one of the smiling tooth bags I assembled.

"Uh-huh."

"What's wrong?" asks Birch.

"Nothing."

"Why does your face look like that then?"

"Like what?"

"Like this." Birch squeezes his eyebrows together and puckers his nose. "Like something smells bad. Or is *something* bothering you?" He stares pointedly at my head.

"Zip it already!" I make sure no one's around to have noticed his less-than-subtle inquiry. "It's Milkshake."

Birch sniffs the gasping dog. "I don't smell anything unusual on Milkshake."

"I don't mean he smells. He's what's bothering me. I have to walk him every day, and I don't really like him very much. It's complicated." I don't tell Birch that Dr. Flossdrop adopted Milkshake to replace my brother, who Birch doesn't know exists, and that she fawns over Milkshake while either ignoring me, punishing me, or making me do chores.

"Oh, OK." Birch pats Milkshake's head and whispers, "Goodbye, buddy."

"*You* can still like him."

"No, that's OK. He is a bit damp." Birch wipes his hands on his plaid shorts. "Actually, I prefer humans to animals, so if I have to make a choice, I choose you." He starts rifling through the goody bag's contents.

I can't help it; I'm kind of flattered. I never thought Birch would say he prefers me to an animal, even if that animal is Milkshake. I mean, my mother certainly doesn't seem to.

Dr. Flossdrop chooses that moment to peek her head into the waiting room to check on her dog. She waves to me and Birch, and then she's gone. I don't even have a chance to say sorry her neighborhood action plan for the meadow isn't happening. Not that my heart would really be in it anyway.

"So, do you want to hang out?" Birch asks, drawing me back. "I really like your aunt Mildred, and Uncle Lou is the best, and now my teeth are clean, but I could use some, like, age-befitting activity."

I consider this for a moment. I've never done the five-dollar trick by myself, but I watched Adam do it plenty of times last summer. I start talking, slowly, words coming out of my mouth, each one a tiny offering. With every word I'm taking another step in the dark, making sure there's nothing sharp-edged I'll bump into.

"OK . . . yeah," I say. "I have an idea. We just need some fishing line."

Birch nods like he is up for any idea I have, but of course we don't have any fishing line. We search our pockets and the reception desk for a substitute. Nothing.

"How about transparent floss?" Birch holds up his goody bag.

"I can't think of a better use for my mom's dental floss," I say. And that's the truth.

I affix a length of floss to a five-dollar bill Birch had, and we scramble behind the waiting room's saloon doors to hide with the other end of the string.

Soon, a patient walks into the waiting room, a man wearing a mustard-colored dress shirt with giant sweat rings under the arms. We see him eye the five-dollar bill lying in the middle of the pink carpet. And we wait to see if he'll make a move for it . . .

15
LOOP

Out on the sidewalk a few minutes later, Birch and I pant like Milkshake and laugh hysterically.

"I can't believe he actually got down on his knees!"

"In his business clothes!"

"And then you tugged the floss."

"And then he fell on his hands."

"And then he grabbed the five bucks."

"But then I tugged it harder."

"And it ripped in half!" we both shout, laughing uncontrollably.

Once we've calmed down enough to walk straight, Birch and I head back to the duplex. We left the torn bill in the office when we tore out of there ourselves.

I have to admit, Birch is growing on me. I didn't think about the bees *once* while we were in Dr. Flossdrop's office together. I almost forgot them entirely. Plus, he chose me over Milkshake. He's kept my bees to himself. He went on a secret mission he didn't know the secret of. And he gave me a spin on that inversion table, which was amazing.

I'm happy for the first time in so long that I almost feel like doing Adam's fancy bow. I mean, that five-dollar-bill trick was just like my best evers with Adam last summer. I remember the last time we pranked someone: a girl Adam's age. I remember how she didn't fall for it, and Adam liked that about her. They even exchanged numbers. She had a triangles tattoo on her wrist that Adam complimented her on. He liked how geometric it was.

Wait a minute.

Triangles tattooed on her wrist — just like the ones from Lou's M. C. Escher LIBERATION poster with triangles and birds.

Birds. Just like the birds tattooed on the girl's shoulder at Starving Artists Movers.

The same drawing.

The same tattoo.

The same girl.

Adam and that girl from last summer worked at Starving Artists Movers together. That's not just any girl. That girl must be Adam's friend. Or maybe even his *girlfriend*.

When this hits me, I almost faint, right there on the sidewalk next to Birch. Luckily, he probably knows CPR — or at least the kind of CPR used on birds.

Adam was full of secrets. Whatever he was doing with Lou's boxing gloves. Wherever he's disappeared to. And that he had a girl friend/girlfriend. He never told me any of that. He met that girl with me last summer and never even mentioned that he saw her again. He might've been working with her this whole last year. Maybe all that time he was showing *her* what was in his secret notebook instead of me.

More secrets. More betrayal when I thought it couldn't get any worse.

Birch notices a change in my mood. I can tell because he's staring at me funny. But I don't say anything. I race to the duplex before he can even ask.

I run straight to Adam's room. My eyes are watering, and my face feels hot. I curl up on his bed. I'm crying as hard as I was laughing after Birch and I did the five-dollar-bill trick just now. My breathing is sad heaves I can't control.

There are some of Adam's drawings taped up on the walls. A couple of vintage magician posters. He's got a collection of stuff — plastic figurines and yo-yos — in piles on his nightstand. Coasters. Receipts with doodles. Mixed-up decks of cards. Nothing that tells me anything about where he is.

I open his nightstand drawer.

There's not much in there. Pay stubs from Starving Artists, matchboxes, a harmonica. But in all the mess is a photo I've never seen before. It's of Adam when he was little, with Dad. It must have been taken a couple of years before I was even born. They're working together in a

123

wood shop full of stuff. They wear matching denim coveralls. Dad leans over Adam, steadying his forearm, helping him hammer a nail into wood.

Dad died before he had the chance to show *me* how to hammer a nail into wood. How to show me anything. But I always had Adam. Having Adam made me feel like I knew Dad — at least a little. Adam was my brother, my best friend, and my connection to our dad all wrapped up into one. Having Adam made it not matter so much that I'd never really met my dad. But now it does matter. Because now I've got nothing I can count on.

I bring the photo to my room down the hall. I slip it in my own nightstand drawer, cushioned by a million skeins of yarn. I need something else to yarn bomb in here besides my alarm clock and bed. I settle on the geometric base of my lamp. I'll use stripes again, this time in muted rainbow colors instead of black and yellow. I can't take any more black and yellow.

As I measure and start knitting, I think about how Adam left me here, all alone, with Dr. Flossdrop and these bees. I think about all the secrets he was keeping, especially this latest one, his girlfriend. About those twice-goodbye blue leather boots. About where he went. More than anything I wonder when — or if — I'll ever hear from him again.

Bees
THE HUMAN

We were angry at the human. Perhaps even more than we were angry at Bee 641 for getting us into this mess. It was easier to be angry than to admit what we really were — scared.

We didn't like how the human smelled. We didn't like the sharp wooden needles she stuck in our hive every once in a while. We even came to detest the sound of her breathing.

We wanted nothing more than to get back at her, but we wouldn't stoop to using our stingers. That would be low. And also, it would be self-sabotage.

Every night when the human climbed in bed, just before she rested her head on her pillow, we rearranged ourselves so we wouldn't be crushed.

We stayed like that for hours. We waited in an uncomfortable position all night long until her head finally came up in the morning, and we could resettle properly again.

While the human slept, a couple of us would break away and hover over her dreaming face in order to come back to the group and give commentary. We were told she looked disturbed. Restless. Worried. Sometimes her chin twitched.

And as much as we tried, it was hard to hold the fact that she was a terrible home against her when we heard how her perturbed chin twitched in her sleep like that. It almost made us feel sorry for her. She wasn't the only one who was worried, restless, and perturbed. It might've been hard to admit, but we could relate.

16
BACKSTITCH

Whoosh.

Lou is at my front door, carrying a package. Mail often gets delivered to the other side of the duplex by accident. Probably has a lot to do with the fact that Dr. Flossdrop has been known to order large quantities of recycled paper — which she uses for neighborhood action flyers — online.

"Zinny!"

"Hi, Lou."

"You can call me Coach, you know that."

"I know," I say. But that's all I say.

"And did you know it's summertime?" asks Lou.

"Of course I know it's summer."

"Oh, well I wasn't sure, what with that hood on your head and being indoors. In my day, I would've been . . . oh, never mind," he says, stopping himself from saying something that's probably inappropriate.

When I don't say anything else, Lou holds out a FROM THE OFFICE OF PHILOMENA FLOSSDROP, D.D.S. sticky note.

"I believe this is for you," he says.

I take the note, which says that I shouldn't walk Milkshake today because he appears fatigued and needs to rest. That's great news because *I* could really use a rest from walking Milkshake — not that Dr. Flossdrop would ever notice that.

"And *this* has your name on it," Lou adds, handing me the package.

"My name? I never get mail."

Then it hits me — maybe it's from Adam! It has to be. Maybe he's sent me something to explain his series of betrayals and restore order to my universe. There's no return address, which confirms my suspicion. I want to shut the door in Lou's face but that would be rude.

"I'm sorry. I have to open this," I tell Lou. "Now."

"All right. Glad to see you're excited about that box. Keep your head up," he says as I start to close the door. "And I mean that. Keep your clavicle open so your neck stays nice and long. Work on that. Consider it your homework."

"Sure," I say, even though I'm not totally sure what my clavicle is.

Once Lou is gone, I open the box with scissors. Inside, there's a smaller package wrapped in brown paper. A note sits on top. I can tell immediately it's not Adam's handwriting. I don't want to read any note that's not from Adam, but I can't stop myself — it's from NML.

Why would they send me something in the mail? I wonder. Is it too awful to give me in person? What mean thing could they pass off as a gift? What could this package contain that will permanently sever our friendship and betray me even more?

I read the note.

Zinnia,

We thought the rattlesnake mascot looked a lot better with that sweater on. Even if we'd known you were the one who did it, we wouldn't have gotten you in trouble. We miss you and hope you'll be friends with us again in eighth grade.

Have a good summer.

Nikki, Margot, and Lupita

I can't believe what I'm reading. They seem to be claiming they *didn't* betray me to the vice principal . . . that someone else saw me knitting and knew it was me. They also seem to be under the impression that *I* was the one who stopped being friends with *them*.

But why should I believe anything they say?

I open the package wrapped in brown paper. It's a skein of yarn. It's charcoal gray, like all my clothes.

They sent me yarn in my favorite color. Which is pretty weird.

Despite my confusion, I immediately want to put it to good use. I take a ceramic cactus Mildred gave me a long time ago from my dresser and start wrapping one cactus arm, then the other, with the gray yarn from NML. I do it again and again and again, then move on to the main part of the cactus until it's all covered too. I cut and tuck the loose end under the bottom of the pot before moving on to my old piggy bank shaped like a robot.

As I wrap, I reach back in my memory and try to figure out if there was a specific moment that NML and I stopped being friends. Some crucial scene to unlock the mystery of when and where and why they deserted me.

The reel that plays in my mind is a collection of scenes, and they're all basically the same. *Me* eating lunch alone against the concrete wall by the back entrance of school. *Me* avoiding *them*. *Me* not telling *them* about my knitting or my parking meter yarn bombs or my plans for Ronny the Rattlesnake. *Me* thinking Adam was my only friend, that no one else could possibly understand.

Yup, Adam. He'd turned eighteen and was working full time at Starving Artist Movers when I started school last year. His arguments with Dr. Flossdrop were escalating. I felt the ground shifting under me at home, tremors of what eventually cracked — that Adam wouldn't be around forever, at least not in the same way he always had. I didn't want anything to change, but I felt Adam drifting away. So I grabbed on harder any way I could. I pretended nothing else mattered. I didn't want anything else to hurt me like Adam's distance did. Like his exit would.

The reel of seventh grade continues to play in my mind, and it's *me* backing away, step by step. *Me*, too scared to take a step in the other direction. Instead of walking toward my friends when I needed them, I walked away.

I wrap and wrap. The yarn feels soft between my thumb and forefinger as my feelings toward my former friends begin to soften too. I wrap until the robot bank is completely covered and looks like a gray, robot-shaped blob.

I guess I did the same thing with the truth about what happened between me and NML — I covered it up. I made myself believe NML were the ones leaving me; that way I could pretend it didn't matter. I could pretend I preferred to be just a Z.

But the truth is, I didn't feel that way — I just felt safer. And now it means I feel all alone.

17
MOVIE NIGHT

The smell of roses surges toward me when I arrive at Aunt Mildred's apartment for movie night. Flower overpowers the cinnamon that's always in the air.

"Zinnia! Action's in the kitchen!"

Mildred's right about action. She's wearing an apron with dancing pizza slices on it, and she's bustling around. There are at least a dozen whitish-pink roses on the counter, their petals mostly unfurled. Mildred is scooping something that smells sweet and creamy.

Three mugs rest on the kitchen table, and for a second I expect to see Adam, just like usual. But the third mug isn't for Adam.

Birch is here, pouring tea into those mugs.

For a moment, my stomach feels like it capsizes, but then it flips right side up again. Despite the fact that I was running away from him the last time I saw him, I'm happy to see Birch. I'm getting used to him being around all the time. I'm even getting used to the bees being around all the time, which is pretty weird. That doesn't mean I don't still *want* them to buzz off though. Because I *definitely* do.

"*Coucou!*" says Mildred. "I see you're still wearing your disguise."

She waves her spoon at my hood, and I give her a look that says, *stop talking about it.* And she does. Because she's Mildred.

"Hi, Zinnia!" says Birch.

"Hi," I say.

"Would you like some tea?" asks Birch, stirring honey into one of the mugs.

"Please," I say. "No honey for me, though."

Birch looks briefly at my hood and winks. He must've picked up the winking thing from Lou.

"I made rose ice cream," says Mildred, swaying while her dainty hands work.

"Wait a minute. We're going to *eat* roses?" I ask.

"Absolutely," says Mildred. "These are organic roses a patient gave me from her garden. She wanted to thank me for teaching her how to use a gum massager to control plaque between visits."

"Actually," says Birch, "a number of flowers are edible. My mom makes tea from dandelions. And sometimes we eat salad with marigold petals thrown in."

Of course naturalist Birch eats marigold petals in his salad. "That sounds pretty weird. Must be a Redwood City thing."

"Hon, you can eat flowers anyplace!" chimes Mildred. "Pansies are *magnifique*! You can even eat *zinnias*!"

I guess it's two against one. And I guess it does smell pretty edible in here.

Birch and I take a seat at the kitchen table, sipping tea and watching Mildred shimmy her hips here and there.

"I'm giving this ice cream a trial run for when Viviana comes over for our date tomorrow night," says Mildred.

"I'll be your ice cream date guinea pig anytime," I say.

"Who's Viviana?" asks Birch.

"She's in my French class. This will be our third date." Mildred does a little spin.

"Well, rose ice cream seems very romantic," says Birch, to which I look at him funny.

"What movie do you two want to watch tonight?" Mildred asks.

"Why don't we watch *Crowd Pleasers*?" asks Birch.

"What's that?"

"It's a reality show."

"That's not a movie," I say.

"No, but it's really great. I've been watching it while Uncle Lou works with his clients. I think you'd like it."

"Birch, I'm sure your program is wonderful, but there are some rules around here," says Mildred. "Only a few, but they're important. Brushing and flossing for one. Dessert." She joins us with pink bowls of pink ice cream. "And watching French films."

I nod my head, affirming Mildred's rules.

"Let's make like root canals and dig in," she says. "I made the ice cream pink by using beet juice!"

I take an obedient bite. After the flower conversation, I know enough not to question ingredients.

We don't end up watching a French movie or any movie at all. Hyper after two bowls of ice cream apiece — delicious and approved for Viviana — we instead decide to play charades in the living room, where there are butterflies on the curtains and cat pillows on the couch. Practically everything's yellow or pink. Adam used to refer to Aunt Mildred's decorating style as "pink, sunshine, and kittens."

Mildred goes first. It's pretty obvious what she's acting out. To me anyway. She walks around on her knees like she's a kid and reaches her hand up in the air, grasping at something. I know the something must be a balloon because I've seen *The Red Balloon*, one of Mildred's favorite French films, with her and Adam a hundred times.

Birch on the other hand has no idea what's going on. Finally I can't take it anymore so I shout the answer, then Mildred and I fill him in.

Birch goes next. He unbuttons the first few buttons of his plaid shirt. This is starting out pretty weird, and I can't help but laugh. Then he gets down on the floor and attempts a one-armed push up. He collapses, but we still get the idea. He's Lou.

It's my turn next. I lie on the couch across the room from Birch and Mildred. I rest my chin on a pillow and breathe loudly through my mouth with my tongue out. I try to look as floppy as possible.

"Milkshake!" they both yell immediately.

It's odd, but I'm glad we're having charades night instead of movie night. After all, things are different now.

Mildred kisses me on the cheek and shakes Birch's hand at nine o'clock on the dot.

"I'm throwing you out like used dental floss," she says. "Let's *soirée* again soon, though!" She blows kisses at Birch and me as we walk out together into the balmy air.

Birch and I go through the gate of Mildred's apartment building. My breath still tastes like roses, and it smells like jasmine out here.

"You must miss your brother," Birch says out of nowhere, completely changing the mood.

My breath catches for a second before I'm able to speak. "What do you mean?"

"Adam, your brother. Lou told me he left the day we met, after you came over for lunch and ice cream."

"Oh." I guess Dr. Flossdrop told Lou. Or maybe Adam told Lou he was going to leave when he borrowed those boxing gloves. That feels even worse.

I start walking down the hill toward Sunrise Boulevard and the duplex again, focusing on the itchiness of the bees, which is slightly more pleasant than hearing that another big secret isn't a secret at all.

"Did he work at Starving Artists Movers?" asks Birch.

"Are you a detective?" I ask, walking faster.

"No. I thought that's what you were — a detective on the hunt for her brother."

"Why didn't you say anything then?"

"I didn't think you wanted to talk about it."

"Well, I don't," I say.

"OK," says Birch.

I count mailboxes as we walk. Mailbox number one has a dolphin on it. Mailbox number two, minimal and metal. Three, four, and five are regular old mailboxes.

I consider everything I know about Birch. How much fun charades was tonight. All the things we've shared by now.

Finally I stop walking and look at him. Birch's eyes still remind me of the ocean, even in the semidarkness.

"OK. Can you keep a secret?" I ask.

"Do birds fly?" Birch looks up as though he's going to see one fly overhead in the murky night sky. "That is, except for some birds that *don't* fly, like ostriches, penguins, turkeys . . ."

"I get the idea."

I try to calm my firecracker heart. Here goes nothing. "Adam didn't just leave. Dr. Flossdrop drove him away. They'd been fighting a lot this past year."

"Whoa. What about?"

"Mostly about how Adam wanted to be an artist and how Dr. Flossdrop wanted him to be a doctor . . . or at least something useful. Maybe a teacher or a community activist."

"Wow." Birch looks engrossed, like he's never had a fight with anyone in his family and this is as fascinating as a baby eaglets' nest.

Then I do something really strange. Perhaps stranger even than having bees on my head. I sit down on the curb, and Birch sits down next to me. And I keep talking. About Adam and Adam leaving. About NML. I tell him they didn't betray me like I said. Like I thought. That they sent me a note and charcoal-gray yarn. I even tell Birch about losing my dad before ever knowing him.

I tell him everything. I take steps toward him instead of away.

Birch is so quiet it's like I'm talking to myself. But in a good way. And then, when I'm done, he looks at me and nods. He doesn't say anything. He's the ocean again. Breathing in and out, there to catch whatever I throw.

Bees

HOPE? WHAT HOPE?

We looked up from our glumness to find flowers right there in front of us. The princess of all flowers — roses! Exquisite, delicious, and even organic roses!

We wasted no time; we rubbed our legs together to warm them up for revelry. Our senses awakened, and blood pulsed through our membranes.

Then the realization set in. Those roses were no longer in the ground, fed by soil. They were just lying there, their stems sad, lifeless sticks. What was left of their pollen was probably stale.

They would be a crummy snack and then what? We'd go right back to where we were. On the human's head with no nectar and no honeycomb and no purpose. Why even bother?

We began to wonder if we'd live out the rest of our days here, the last of our line. If we'd been delusional to ever think otherwise. If the risk we'd taken had been our downfall, a danger we should never have hazarded.

We wondered if this *was the only sad destiny we'd ever get. And if we had no one to blame but ourselves.*

After the rose incident, despair swept the hive.

The queen gave inspirational speeches. She ordered her attendants to tell jokes.

But it was too late.

Heads hung. Mandibles drooped. Compound eyes dulled.

We slept. We slept only to be unconscious. To escape.

18
OPERATION MILKSHAKE

When I arrive at Dr. Flossdrop's office to pick up Milkshake for his daily walk — my never-ending punishment for the Ronny yarn bomb — he looks worse than usual. His tongue hangs farther out of his mouth, and he lies on the pink carpet even more pathetically.

I attach the leash to Milkshake's collar, and he looks disappointed that I'm the one here to walk him again this morning. Or maybe I'm reading too much into it.

Before I can coax Milkshake out of his position on the floor, a man bursts in, holding his face with both hands.

"May I help you?" I ask. While I don't work here, I *am* related to the dentist and dental assistant. Plus I'm the only other person in the waiting room.

"I'm in a *lot* of pain. *A lot* of pain," says the man.

Somehow having sensed someone in need, Mildred barrels through the saloon doors. She whisks the man back through them. I can still hear him talking about pain as they move farther down the hall. Pain when he eats, pain when he sleeps, a painful bubble on his gum that started oozing pus this morning. *Gross.*

I want to get out of here as soon as possible, which means convincing Milkshake to actually stand up, but Milkshake is wheezing. I mean, even more than normal. This is more like a wheeze-cough, like he's a cat with a hairball stuck in his throat instead of a small, asthmatic terrier.

Milkshake looks up at me, his tongue more grape than strawberry like it usually is. His eyes are dark and glossy and suffering. And the coughing's getting worse. A lot worse.

I remove the leash and pick him up, pretending he's a ball of yarn instead of Milkshake. He's surprisingly soft while somehow also being bony and damp. His body quakes and yes, he dribbles a little urine onto the sleeve of my hoodie.

I run to the exam room.

Dr. Flossdrop stands above the man in pain, shining a small, mirrored light into his mouth. The man lies back in the chair, jaw agape. Mildred, in her scrubs adorned with champagne glasses, crouches next to the patient, giving his shoulder a tender squeeze. Classical music reverberates through the room.

"I'm sorry," I say. "You're busy. It's just . . . Milkshake. Something's wrong." I hold him out like a platter.

Dr. Flossdrop takes one look at Milkshake and, waving her tiny flashlight in the air, pronounces, "Asthma attack!"

Mildred and the man burst into chaotic action. Mildred runs to soothe the dog. The man takes off his paper towel bib and offers it in Milkshake's direction as though it's a dog inhaler and not a useless paper towel bib.

Dr. Flossdrop's action is clear and has purpose, though. She starts telling me what to do.

"Zinnia, go to the vet. I'm counting on you. I have to stay here and perform an emergency root canal or this man's infection could spread to his jaw or neck."

The patient, who was refastening his paper towel bib, freezes when he hears this information.

But I don't freeze. I go forth with my mission while Mildred finishes refastening the man's bib, trying to convince him an emergency root canal won't be as bad as it sounds.

I carry Milkshake's shivering body like I totally know what I'm doing. I have so many thoughts at once:

1. Dr. Flossdrop will disown me or curse me to a life of purposelessness if anything happens to her precious Milkshake.

2. Since I have bees on my head, I'm kind of part of the animal world and owe it some protection.

3. Perhaps because Milkshake is Adam's replacement or because of all the time we've spent together on walks, I might actually care what happens to Dr. Flossdrop's dog.

It seems like I walk blocks and blocks, way past the meadow, before the vet's office appears before me across the street. But finally, there it is: CREATURES LARGE AND SMALL VETERINARY HOSPITAL.

I start to cross the street, but about halfway there, I trip over a little crater in the asphalt. The only thing I pay attention to is Milkshake. I can't drop this dog. And I don't. But I do collapse on the pavement and bang my elbow really hard.

My hood drops back a little, but my only concern is keeping Milkshake cradled in my arms. He seems unperturbed. I think he's fallen asleep. Or passed out. Or worse.

Then one of his eyes opens, and he looks up at me before I have a chance to fix my hood. And with that one eye open for a couple of seconds, I see Milkshake see the bees. Now it really feels like we're in this thing together.

I scramble to my feet and push open the door once I reach it.

"This dog is having an asthma attack. Can you save this dog?" I ask the veterinary helpers in the reception area. They wear scrubs like Mildred's, but not as colorful.

Someone quickly lifts Milkshake from my arms and whisks him back to an exam room. I take a seat. It's much quieter and calmer here than Dr. Flossdrop's office. There are dim lamps on the desk. Some kind of nature music with birds chirping is playing. Of course, I think of Birch.

This is not a typical veterinary office. It's so peaceful it's making me drowsy.

I slump in a chair and close my eyes.

A long time later I feel a mysterious hand tap my shoulder.

It's the veterinarian's hand. She wears jeans and a maroon lab coat over a stretchy cotton shirt. She sits down next to me and, clearly thinking Milkshake is my beloved pet, keeps her hand on my shoulder as she speaks to me in a soft voice.

"Your dog is going to be OK, but he's in bad shape right now. I've run some tests."

"What do the tests say?" I ask, my own hands trembling in a way that reminds me of Milkshake himself.

"It's not an asthma attack. Milkshake's breathing problem has to do with his windpipe. We can probably avoid surgery by treating him with medication and acupuncture."

For a second all I can think about is how weird it is to hear that Dr. Flossdrop was wrong about something. But then I process what the vet said.

"You mean you're going to stick needles in him? In his throat?"

"Yes, needles. No, not in his throat. Don't worry," she says, reassuring me, "the acupuncture needles don't hurt."

I guess I looked worried. I guess I was.

"Will it help?" I ask.

"We sure hope so."

I look around at the lamps. More nature music is playing, this time a river lapping at rocks and spilling over a waterfall.

"Go ahead and treat Milkshake," I say.

"All right. Just relax," she assures me.

And seconds later, I'm alone again.

"Come to Mama!!" Dr. Flossdrop oozes in her sugary, reserved-for-Milkshake voice, lifting the now normally breathing (aka steadily wheezing) dog from my arms.

I try to hand over the medicine Milkshake is supposed to take, but Dr. Flossdrop is too busy celebrating. She holds the dog up in the air like he's a victorious athlete after a canine competition. Mildred stands nearby, holding one tiny hand to her heart.

"Zinnia! You saved my baby!" Dr. Flossdrop squeals, looking from Milkshake to me. Apparently she doesn't notice the strangeness of calling the dog her baby in the presence of her actual child.

"It was really the veterinarian," I say. "She used acupuncture to help calm Milkshake's breathing. There's medication too."

Dr. Flossdrop marches over and gives me the biggest hug I have ever received from her. It's not exactly what you'd call a cinnamon-roll hug, but it's not quite as stiff as a metallic robot-dentist either.

"Thank you, Zin. You rescued Milkshake. I'm so proud of you."

I shrug, even though a tight smile tugs at my lips. It feels good that she's treating me like a dog-saving hero, but I can't help but wonder what she'd say if the mission hadn't succeeded, if I hadn't turned out to be useful today.

Despite usefulness being her number one concern, Milkshake's not even a little bit useful and Dr. Flossdrop doesn't seem to care. I wish my mom were ever half as excited about me as she *always* is about Milkshake. One thing's for sure: Dr. Flossdrop loves that do-nothing little dog.

19
ZINGER

Maybe this is what Dr. Flossdrop feels like when she does neighborhood action. A big, satisfying sense of accomplishment. Even though it was Milkshake I helped and not, like, a more developed lifeform. Say a lizard or houseplant.

I peek past the oleander hedge out in front of the duplex when I get there. There's the yard, same as usual, with Dr. Flossdrop's cactuses and succulents and other spiny, drought-tolerant plants. And then there's Birch.

He looks normal in that he's wearing plaid, but not normal in that he's doing this strange dance routine around the yard. It takes me a minute to realize it's not actually a dance routine; it's the sidestep Lou always assigns his clients. The one I sometimes hear him chanting about from our side of the duplex: "Longer step, tummy tight, don't forget to pump that knee!"

But Birch's long-legged sidesteps are exaggerated, which makes it look like he's dancing. Plus he's trying to avoid getting stuck by a spiny plant as he does the routine, which makes it extra entertaining. He stops sidestepping when he hears me laugh.

"What are you up to?" asks Birch. "Besides laughing at me."

"Going to Scoops. I just rescued Milkshake from a breathing attack, and I want to celebrate. Wanna come?"

Birch, of course, accepts.

"I'm going to run inside for a minute first," I say. Saving a dog makes a person thirsty, and I need some water. "Do you want to come in and wait?"

Birch has never been inside our half of the duplex. But he accepts this invitation as well.

When I come out of the kitchen with two glasses of water, Birch is in the doorway of my bedroom. His mouth is open a little bit like it was when I showed him the bees.

"Whoa," he says.

It's been two and a half weeks, and I've managed to cover almost my entire room in yarn, either knit or just wrapped: the wooden parts of my bed; my nightstand, lamp, and alarm clock; everything on my dresser, including the cactus, the piggy bank, a couple of wooden boxes, a mug of pens, and some books. I've even wrapped the light fixture hanging from the ceiling above my bed with yarn and dangled a garland with pompoms from it.

"What is this?" asks Birch, taking the glass from me. "It's like, like . . . your whole room molted a multicolored sweater."

"It's called yarn bombing. And that's exactly how I think of it!"

"It's amazing," says Birch.

"Thank you." I take a sip from my own glass since it feels like my mouth is as filled with wool as my room. Pretty weird, but it's nice to share my yarn bombing with someone else, even if that someone isn't Adam.

And if I'm perfectly honest with myself, I'm glad that someone is Birch.

Birch orders durian when we get to Scoops.

"What's durian?" I ask.

"It's a Southeast Asian fruit that supposedly smells really bad."

"And you want to eat it as an ice-cream flavor?"

"I don't think the fruit *inside* smells bad. Plus I've never tasted it." Birch smiles like he's on the greatest adventure of his life.

I order lavender lemon zinger because I'm now accustomed to eating flowery ice cream thanks to Mildred. There's no way I'm willing to risk ordering mint chocolate chip again. Not after what happened last time I was here. It feels like forever ago that the bees landed, even though it's only been eighteen days — but who's counting?

I push the thought from my mind and focus on the ice cream I'm ordering. It's swirls of purple and yellow and cream. I love how the spoon is more like a paddle than a spoon. I also love that they have a TV here. Since Dr. Flossdrop will never let us have one, it makes enjoying ice cream here all the more decadent.

Birch and I each pay and are walking away from the cash register when a teenage girl comes in with her friend. But it's not just any teenage girl.

It's Adam's girlfriend.

I'd recognize her anywhere now. Her straight dark ponytail, the M. C. Escher birds drawn on the back of her neck that continue down her shoulder.

I immediately throw my cone and cup and spoon in the trash and march right over to her. I vaguely hear Birch asking me why I just did that, but I keep walking rather than answer.

Adam's girlfriend is talking to a friend, but when a random twelve-year-old comes over, she gives me her full attention. "Zinnia?" she says.

OK, so maybe I'm not a random twelve-year-old to her. Maybe Adam actually mentioned me after all. Maybe she remembers me from the five-dollar-bill trick last summer, or Adam showed her a picture of me on his phone before he left.

I'm a little thrown that she recognized me, but I waste no time on pleasantries. "Do you know where Adam is?"

Girlfriend nods.

"Where then?"

"I promised I wouldn't tell anyone," she says, not meeting my eyes. She starts twirling her super-long ponytail in her hand.

"Not even *me*?" I ask.

There's no answer, but she winces a little and shakes her head.

I look from the girl's ponytail to her T-shirt-covered shoulder, down her arm to where her tattoo changes from birds to triangles. I feel *myself* transforming into a triangle. A gray, wavy triangle balancing on one point. Because this stranger knows where Adam is, and I don't. He told her and not me.

Suddenly the whole world seems even shakier and more uncertain and upside down. And not in an inversion-table, best-ever kind of way. Not that way at all.

As if things couldn't get any worse, when Birch and I are walking home, I see NML heading toward us on the sidewalk. It's near the spot where the bees took up residence in my hair, and I can't help but think that maybe this stretch of Sunrise Boulevard is cursed.

But then, maybe it's just anywhere I go that's cursed.

I'm run-walking, and Birch is slightly behind me, trying to keep up, yelling ahead about how good durian tastes despite the rumors about how pungent it smells. I can hear him hypothesizing that Scoops probably added a lot of sugar to the ice cream version, but I'm too busy fuming to respond. I can't stop thinking about Adam's girlfriend refusing to tell me where he is and, even worse, knowing that she knows and I don't and that's how Adam wants it.

So when I see NML, everything in my body speeds up even more. My lungs are inhaling and exhaling in this frantic turbo pattern that's impossible to ignore but out of my control. I feel like Milkshake having his breathing attack earlier today. Maybe breathing attacks are contagious from dogs to humans.

"Durian ice cream is hard to pin down," Birch is saying, still concentrating on his culinary commentary and the spoon heading toward his mouth. "Maybe it tastes a tiny bit like butterscotch."

"Hurry," I say, grabbing Birch mid-bite and dragging him along with me between the sneaker and art supply stores. There's the tiniest cutout here, barely the size of an elevator. I pull us both inside, wishing desperately it had a front door so I could shut it. Or that it was like the elevator in *Charlie and the Chocolate Factory* so we could blast off somewhere before NML walk by.

"No, it tastes like caramel maybe," Birch is saying. "Or mango. But oddly kind of like cooked onions, too." He's apparently in an entirely different story than I am right now.

I place Birch in front of me and crouch down behind him and try to get my breathing to slow. Birch takes another bite and then *finally* seems to realize what's happening.

"Are you hiding?" he asks.

"Yes," I say. "And so are you. Shhhh."

"Who are we hiding from?"

"NML."

"But why? I thought you said you were wrong about NML."

"Shhhh," I say again. "I *was* wrong. But . . . I don't know. I'm not ready, OK? I'm not ready to see them, and today is not the right day after everything that's happened, and I'm tired and . . ."

"Shhhh," says Birch.

"Why are you shushing *me*?" I ask, not whispering anymore.

"Because NML are about to walk by, and I assumed you didn't want them to hear you. Isn't that why you're hiding?"

"Yes. Thank you. Shhhh," I say one final time.

I can see NML out there, passing by. I pull Birch's elbow so he turns around to face me, and he acts like he's inspecting the paint job on the wall. I hide behind his plaidness, making myself as small as I possibly can.

It's stifling hiding back here with the bees under my hood, but in another few seconds NML have passed by and are gone. I know because Birch says, "They're gone" way too loud.

We step out, and Birch heads over to a trash can to throw out his ice cream cup and spoon. When he comes back to join me, my lungs are finally breathing at a somewhat normal speed, taking in regular amounts of oxygen.

"Maybe I should've said hello," I say. "I panicked."

"I'm sure you'll have another chance to see them again," says Birch. "You've seen them twice now this summer, right?"

"I guess so," I say, relief and regret dueling to take the lead on how I should feel right now.

"Chin up," says Birch, another phrase I'm not familiar with. It sounds like something Lou would say. It's nice.

I try to hold my chin up the tiniest bit. But it feels pretty hard when there's so much to weigh me down.

Bees
RECREATION

One of the bees called a meeting. Remarkably, it wasn't to grumble about Bee 641 or anything else. It was about a new way for us to combat despair and pass the time. The bee called it breakdancing.

We formed a circle as instructed. One bee took her place in the middle while the rest watched, swaying our abdomens rhythmically behind us. She showed us each move, so we could get the hang of it.

The six-legged moonwalk.

The head spin.

The robot. (Bees are especially well-suited for this move, as we love doing things with precision.)

Everyone laughed at the worm. We'd met a few worms in our day, and imitating them was quite satisfying.

We breakdanced with fervor. With four thousand bees, it took a long time for everyone to get their turn in the circle. Oh, but we had fun. We celebrated a couple of weddings this way. We imagined the possibility of celebrating a birth, too, if things were to change. We felt alive with culture and togetherness. The queen looked on, beaming at the unity of her hive in the midst of hardship.

The problem was we were desperately hungry again after all that breakdancing, which only served to reignite the crankiness of our melancholy.

20
STITCH

Birch and I are at the meadow to bird-watch. He says it will help get my mind off Adam and his girlfriend and the zing of betrayal. Also, the embarrassing way I hid from NML — again.

A lot of people are at the meadow today, picnicking and whatnot. I knit while Birch bird-watches. The bees scurry around under my hood, like thunder in a cloud.

When I'm done knitting, I ask Birch if I can borrow his binoculars.

"Close your eyes," I tell him.

He does, without question, because he's Birch.

I slip the white knit sleeve I brought with me around one of the lens tubes. The sleeve I've been working on, which is black, I bind off, wrap around the other tube, and then close its seam as quickly as I can.

I used my arm as a measurement for how big around to make these when I planned this last night, and I'm relieved to see I was close. It now looks like Birch's binoculars are wearing loosely knit wristbands. I made one black and one white to represent a soccer ball, a good luck charm to help him make the team.

"OK, you can open your eyes now," I say, holding out the binocular strap.

Birch takes the binoculars and turns them over and around, examining them in all directions. "No way! Yarn bomb? For me?"

"Yarn bomb for you. Well, kind of like binocular socks for you in this case."

"Lens warmers."

I smile. "Yeah, something like that."

"Everyone in my bird-watching club is going to love these," he says. "They're going to be so jealous."

"I wouldn't go that far."

"I would," says Birch, who immediately puts the binoculars back on and stares through them.

After that we wait for something bird-watch-y to happen while Birch tells me more than I could ever have wanted to know about feathers, eggs, and wings. I get a whiff of sweat and grass and something else like peppermint sitting this close to him.

We wait some more.

I thread my shoelaces through my fingers and count picnicking people. When I get to 22 something finally happens.

Birch drops his cozied lenses to hang around his neck, his eyes, with faint circles around them, stretched out in wonder. "Look, look!" he says.

"What?"

He puts the binoculars up to my face.

"Look!" he says again.

"Where?" I point them around in all directions. There's tall grass, there are people, there's sky, and there are houses over there, farther away.

And then there it is. This beautiful bird. Huge but slender. It's sleek and tall and graceful. Light gray with flecks of

ZINNIA AND THE BEES

dark on its wings. It's got one long feather jutting out from the back of its head. It flies above the meadow and then farther away and out of sight.

"What was that?" I ask Birch.

"A great blue heron."

"Wow."

"Yeah," he says.

"I've never seen one before. Where do they live?"

"They need to be near water, so that one's probably headed to the river."

"Wow," I say. "I get it."

"Get what?" asks Birch.

"Bird-watching. I get it."

"Yeah," says Birch. "And I get yarn bombing."

And that's when I get something else. Blue herons need to be near water, so they fly over the city to get to the trickle of a river a few miles away. What about bees? What might bees need to be near to make *them* fly away? I feel pretty silly for not figuring this out already. I'm just not sure exactly what to do about it. Yet.

Bees
REPORTS

We couldn't sustain the breakdancing. Our elbows got sore, and our legs ached, not to mention the lack of nutrition to support such a physically demanding activity.

We had nothing to eat. We had nothing to do. And nothing ever happened.

Once in a while a report was given to the queen, but they were always pointless and one of the following:

Complaints about the living conditions.

Complaints about hunger.

Accusations against another bee of something petty, such as having looked at you funny.

Needless to say, the queen stopped listening to reports.

21

CLICK

The day after Birch and I go bird-watching, I arrive at Lou's to find the TV blaring. That way he can still hear it while he does push-ups that include very heavy breaths on each up. He's right there on the kitchen floor, not even worried about how he looks or sounds.

"I came to ask for your help with something," I tell Birch, who's watching TV from his seat at the kitchen table. "I think I have an idea for how to get rid of — "

"What did you say?" he interrupts. "I can't hear you."

"I have an idea — "

"Hold on. This is it!" says Birch.

"What?" I'm officially full-on yelling above the TV now.

"This is that show I was telling you and Mildred about," says Birch. He's yelling now too.

"What show?"

"The one I watch when Uncle Lou's busy with his clients. Or doing push-ups." Birch points to Lou, still pushing-up and grunting, on the floor. *"Crowd Pleasers."*

"Sounds gross," I yell-say.

"It's not gross," says Birch. "It's en*gross*ing." He slides a chair out from Lou's kitchen table and gestures for me to sit down next to him.

I do because, well, I'm here.

The *Crowd Pleasers* opener is still going. Now that it's in front of me, this show's not what I thought it would be — food or fashion or something else boring. The camera keeps flashing to all these street performers. There are some celebrity judges, but I think the scoring is based mostly on how crowds on the street react to each performance. Whether they clap and stick around and throw tips or just keep moving down the sidewalk.

After the opening, the first real bit comes on. It's a few shots of a musician playing the cello. Then there's a puppeteer, but it's just a second on the screen, like a recap. Her puppet is a strange creature riding a horse.

The next performer's clip starts, and it's not just a recap. He's actually performing for people on the street. He's got clown face paint on, along with a hat and mime outfit, and the banner at the bottom of the screen says this competitor's name is Ace.

Face-paint guy is in front of a subway station somewhere. He's holding a helium balloon by a long string. Only it's not a regular helium balloon. This one is super big, red, and perfectly round. It reminds me of Mildred's French movie, *The Red Balloon*, only much, *much* larger than that one.

Ace paces the street with the balloon floating above him. He looks like a mime crossed with a clown crossed with a modern dancer. He lets the balloon lead him along, eventually dancing with it like it's his partner. Sometimes he eases up on the balloon string and pretends to be dragged along by the big red orb. Sometimes he twirls and leaps and then falls to the ground, taking the string down with him so the balloon softly bounces on the pavement.

I'm mesmerized. I forget where I am. It's like by watching this balloon-toting performer, I'm taking flight with him and his helium balloon. I forget everything else, just like when I'm knitting. My hands are sweaty on the kitchen table, but I can't move them. On TV, a couple of onlookers appear to be wiping their eyes at Ace's performance.

Ace glides over to a neon-pink mini teeter-totter with a pink pineapple balanced on one end. He jumps on the long, empty side — *clack!* — and the pineapple flies off the plank. It arcs up, up, up, headed straight for the huge red balloon. The pineapple flies into it, through it, and lands with a thud on the sidewalk, then rolls away. Meanwhile, the balloon pops, erupting confetti all over Ace, the street, the people.

Everyone on TV gasps at the confetti-pop and then applauds. Birch and I do the same. We're clapping, right there in Lou's kitchen.

"What happened?" says Lou, breaking my trance.

"Ace just happened," says Birch.

"Ah," says Lou, retrieving a sports drink from the fridge, but never looking at the screen. He seems to enjoy listening to TV rather than watching it.

When Lou leaves the kitchen, Birch gets up for a second and turns the volume to a normal level. Then he sits down again, and we watch Ace take in all the applause from the crowd, smiling his big, red-outlined smile.

Then Ace bows. And that's when I know.

It's a fancy bow, complete with hand twirling and gesturing and one leg out in front. It's Adam's bow.

It's Adam.

It has to be.

Suddenly I can't believe I didn't figure it out the first moment I saw this. It has Adam written all over it.

"Adam," I whisper. "It's Adam."

I'm not floating like a balloon anymore. There's a jarring cut to a commercial for cat food, and I zoom down to the ground. Way down.

"That's your brother?" asks Birch, but I can't answer. I give a weak nod.

This is what Adam was planning in his notebook all year without me. This was the big secret he was already keeping. Adam was planning to perform on a reality show. A show that Lou plays in his kitchen. That Birch knows about. That Adam's girlfriend definitely knows about.

And not only that, everyone who watches this show knows where Adam is. Or at least some eighteen-year-old face-painted street performer calling himself Ace. They've known since the show started. While I, his sister, didn't know.

I can't believe I looked for him in our neighborhood — at the meadow, and Scoops, and Starving Artists Movers. This whole time he's been who-knows-where, performing on some TV show in front of the entire country. Why didn't he just tell me? I could've kept his secret the same way his girlfriend did. I could've been watching and rooting for him too.

Shame runs hotly through my body, from my bee-ridden head to my feet. Adam's betrayal feels so much worse than I ever could've imagined. It feels bigger, more public, more important. He didn't just go off to art school or something; he went on national television. Who doesn't tell their own sister when they do that?

Well, forget it. I guess I don't need to search for him anymore or even think about him anymore. Mission accomplished. He's on TV! And I'm doomed to have bees on my head and no big brother or best friend forever.

I feel like I'm going to explode. I jump up from the table and run for Lou's door. Past that annoying poster in the hallway with that awful quote about challenges not having power over you. I hate that poster.

Turning the knob, going under the pull-up bar, leaving the door open behind me. Running down the stairs, across the prickly yard, up my own stairs.

I hear Birch calling after me, but I don't stop.

Finally, when I reach my front door, I turn. "Why didn't you tell me about that show?" I yell at him. "I could've figured out Adam was on it sooner!"

"I tried," says Birch, standing in the middle of the yard between Lou's place and mine. "I didn't know that was your brother."

"I can't believe Adam's girlfriend knew and wouldn't tell me. That she let me find out like that!"

"I'm sorry, Zinnia," says Birch, but I can barely hear him through my own hurt, bewildered fog.

"And Adam. Adam's the worst. He broke . . . everything." My voice breaks too when I say that.

"Maybe he was *going* to tell you. Maybe he just needed to do that on his own first. He's got something special with that performance. I can sort of see why he would leave for that."

And that's when I know. Adam hasn't broken absolutely everything, because something else breaks inside me. My heart, my spirit, something that hurts really, really bad. Birch did that.

"You know what, Birch?" I yell. It's not the yelling-over-the-TV kind of yelling like back at Lou's. This yelling is louder and growlier and as ugly as I can make it. "You don't get anything. You're too open. Too trusting. Naive. It's no wonder you don't have any friends back in Redwood City. You're just an uncoordinated . . ."

I don't know what terrible name to call him. So instead I let the *whoosh* of the front door finish my sentence. Then I open it again, just a crack, to ugly-yell through.

"And I bet you'll never make the soccer team!"

I slam the door so fast and loud that it doesn't even *whoosh*.

I wait on the inside of the door, staring at it like my stare can melt it. Then, finally, I hear Lou's door close. But it doesn't slam like mine did. It shuts with a tiny click that sounds louder than my slam did, at least to me. It sounds final, like after everything, I've finally gone too far.

22
DR. FLOSSDROP

I turn around to see Dr. Flossdrop at the kitchen table sending neighborhood action emails on her laptop. "What was that about?" she asks.

It turns out my mom actually *does* pay attention every once in a while. Apparently at the worst possible moments.

"Nothing."

"Does this have to do with why you weren't there to collect Milkshake for his walk today? I was disappointed you never showed up at the office."

"Maybe there are more important things going on than walking perfect little Milkshake!" I snap.

"What's gotten into you, Zinnia? Do you have another ear infection?"

"Mom, there's not a medical explanation for *everything*. Ugh."

"What is it then?" Dr. Flossdrop pushes her chair away from the kitchen table and smooths her bun. Then she stares at me.

Everything in me wants to keep being mean to anyone in my path. Especially Dr. Flossdrop, who only cares about neighborhood action and Milkshake, who's the whole reason Adam left and kept this big secret. The wheel of my mind spins, looking for the cruelest possible place to stop.

"Adam's on television," I say.

Dr. Flossdrop can't stand television.

"He's on a show called *Crowd Pleasers*."

Dr. Flossdrop can't stand anything artistic and useless and fun.

"Oh," I add. "And he has a secret girlfriend too."

"That can't be true," says Dr. Flossdrop. Her back straightens in her chair. "Someone would have told me. My patients must know about this show."

"Why would they talk to *you* about a TV show? You're the last person anyone would talk to about TV. And besides, Adam's wearing face paint and going by the name Ace. He's pretty unrecognizable. Nobody would know it's him."

Red blotches bloom on Dr. Flossdrop's cheeks, then on her chin and forehead. If her bun could flush, it would be turning red too. She looks so angry I'm not sure *what* she's going to do. Scream. Flail. Destroy the kitchen by way of those metal, beak-shaped, tooth-scraper things. I wonder if she might literally blast off from her chair like a rocket.

That's my cue to turn around and retreat. I head for cover in my room.

She doesn't even yell after me to come back.

I sit on my bed, alone except for the bees, their tickly itch a constant reminder that everything is wonky and wrong, including how mean I was to Birch a couple of minutes ago.

I grab one end of my super-giant, multicolored never-ending scarf. I knit. Loop after loop after loop. But for once, knitting doesn't even help.

That's when I hear something.

I put down my never-ending scarf and slowly turn the knob to peek out the door. I can see my mom out there in the dim living room.

Instead of having blasted off like a rocket, Dr. Flossdrop's body is soft and slumped in her chair.

She looks like an empty, crumpled-up black shirt. Elbows collapsed on knees, face collapsed on hands. Strands of hair have fallen loose from her bun. Her back shakes.

The sound I heard is sobbing. And I've barely heard Dr. Flossdrop sniffle before.

I'm astonished.

Shocked.

Guilty.

Sad.

When she finally stops crying, Dr. Flossdrop looks up at me where I stand. Milkshake wobbles into the room and nudges Dr. Flossdrop's clogs. I walk closer and swipe my mom's back in circles, the way Mildred would. When I stop swiping, she starts talking.

"It's my fault," she says. "I drove Adam away."

I don't know what to say. She's finally saying what I've been thinking for weeks. But now that she's the one admitting it — and crying about it — it doesn't feel so great. Plus, it's right then that I notice she's been drinking coffee out of the mug I yarn bombed.

"It's all my fault," she says again. "I shouldn't have nagged him. More than nagged. Pressured. Yelled. Pestered. I should've trusted him. If I'd supported him, he wouldn't have had to keep all this a secret. We wouldn't all have suffered. *You* wouldn't have had to suffer so much."

Dr. Flossdrop gestures at her laptop, and that's when I see she's looked up a clip of Ace online. That's what made her start crying — watching a video of Adam perform on *Crowd Pleasers*.

"He's really talented," says Dr. Flossdrop.

"That's Adam," I say. "A true artist."

Saying it out loud makes me understand him a little better. It maybe even changes how I see the show. Less like deception. More like destiny.

"So why did you then? Pester him and fight and all that?"

"Can I tell you something?" she asks.

I feel dizzy from this roller-coaster of an afternoon, but I say yes anyway. My mom never tells me anything, so I'm all ears.

"I've been so worried about him since he left. I didn't know where he was, and I knew he'd gone for some reason he couldn't tell me. I felt like I'd failed. I felt powerless."

"Me too."

"I thought I could take my mind off it if I threw myself into whatever else would fill my time and thoughts. Because that's what I do."

"You mean being useful?"

First Dr. Flossdrop looks surprised, but then she shakes her head a little. "I guess I'm pretty predictable. Yes, useful. Exactly." She keeps talking. "I've never really explained what it was like when your dad got sick. I felt powerless then, too. Disoriented. Useless. I had to watch him deteriorate, and there was nothing I could do. After I lost him . . . I just didn't want to feel that way again. I thought if I made myself useful — to my patients, to the neighborhood — I wouldn't."

I look down at Milkshake then, something Mom *could* save.

"Seeing Adam become an adult . . . well, I guess I felt like I was losing him a little bit too. He's so much like your dad. Good at card tricks. Didn't mind attention. Your dad was an artist too. Your knitting and Adam's, well, whatever you call it, reminds me of him. When I realized Adam was really growing up, becoming his own person in a way I couldn't predict or control, I felt helpless again. I thought if I could somehow make him practical, like me, I could protect him. Keep him safe. I focused my energy on something other than how I really felt. Which is, a lot of the time, scared."

Hearing my mother talk, I feel disoriented. I've never thought of her as having feelings — let alone being afraid. What's even more disorienting is that what Dr. Flossdrop is saying makes me think of myself. The way I've tried to protect myself from getting hurt by pretending I don't care — about NML, about Birch. By knitting in order to distract myself from everything else.

Is it possible that despite how she acts, Dr. Flossdrop actually cares about *me*?

"I'm so sorry," she says. "I regret not being there for you. I should've been."

Dr. Flossdrop looks exhausted. She reaches up and rubs her forehead. Then she plucks some strange clip from her bun. It unravels until there she is before me, Dr. Philomena Flossdrop, D.D.S., my mother, luminary of usefulness, with her hair down.

And what's pretty weird is that it looks a lot like mine.

Dr. Flossdrop's slicked-back bun has been concealing a thick bouquet of curls. Just like her usefulness has been concealing her fear. Fear of losing what she cares about. The way she lost Dad.

I'm not mad at her about Adam leaving anymore. I'm not really mad at her about anything — at least not too mad. Instead, it's like Dr. Flossdrop makes more sense. An X-ray I can finally read.

I leave her out here by herself, but only for a minute. I go back to my bedroom. I dig out those blue work boots from under my bed. I take one in each hand, holding on by the laces, frayed and dusty. I sweep Mom's laptop out of the way and put the boots on the table. I sit down and even let Milkshake crawl into my lap. We stay like that. Me, Dr. Flossdrop, and the blue boots that Dad and Adam have worn. It's almost like we're all together as a family.

"I think Adam *is* useful," I say, thinking about everyone on TV smiling and crying at his performance. Thinking about all the times he's been useful to me.

Dr. Flossdrop nods, her eyes still misted. "You're right. He is."

"I miss him," I say.

"Me too." She pauses. "Zin, I want to make sure I don't miss you, OK?"

I pick up a pen and one of her FROM THE OFFICE OF PHILOMENA FLOSSDROP, D.D.S. sticky notes and write one word.

OK.

Dr. Flossdrop reaches out to take my hand, the one that was holding the pen, and squeezes it. I squeeze back.

Who cares how we got here? All I care about is that we've already missed enough.

Bees
EXISTENCE

We remembered what the stars looked like. How they used to twinkle above us at the end of a day spent bounding from flower to flower at an orchard. We remembered gazing up at those stars for a moment before gathering back at the wooden hive to dream of a future in which we were free.

That future had eluded us, and we dared to imagine what must be written in those unseen stars for us now.

It was difficult, but we began the process of accepting our fate, that the rest of our days on this Earth would be spent here, on the human's head. We shared our feelings. We joined our antennae in solidarity. We decided to pass what time we had left by tickling one another's microscopic hairs in order to connect, to feel something, to bring meaning to our remaining moments. To giggle our way into oblivion.

23
PEACE OFFERING

The afternoon sun is hot and bright. So hot and bright, in fact, I wonder if I should just turn around and go back home for some shade.

But I'm already here, standing in front of Lou's ERGO-NOMICALLY CORRECT sign. Both of my hands are occupied with a heavy jar, so I consider knocking on the door with my forehead. But before I have to resort to that, it opens from inside. And there's Lou.

"Hey, Zinny! The hooded girl with her head down!"

"Hi, Lou."

"When are you gonna call me Coach?"

I ignore that. "Is Birch here?"

"Yeah, he's in the equipment room. But he's not feeling too great."

"Is he sick?"

"Nah. I don't think so, but his sidesteps have been off, and he's spending a lot of time staring out the window at flying beetles the last couple of days. Kid's just like his parents when it comes to creatures. You know anything about this funk he's in?"

He winks, and I look away.

Lou keeps talking while ushering me through the door. "Kid needs humans in his life. You've done him a lot of good so far this summer, you know that? Birch likes you as much as I like good alignment."

I take a tentative step down the hallway, moving in the opposite direction of Lou's loud, embarrassing voice.

"Atta girl!" Lou slaps my shoulder so hard I lose my balance from the force and stumble. "I was just going to do some pull-ups," he says.

Big surprise.

"I'll be out here. Take your time."

I round the corner into Lou's equipment room. The soles of Birch's sneakers are all I can see of him, because he's currently lying upside down on the inversion table.

I come closer and can hear him breathing really deeply. I bend down to peek at his face, and his eyes are closed. He might be asleep.

It would be a lot easier to just leave, but I know Lou would tell him I was here. So instead I say, "Hi."

Birch's eyes spring open, and he quickly propels the table to vertical. I can now see his whole plaid self.

"Hi," he says, but he's shaking his head a little, and his face is red. "I was experimenting with what it would be like to be a bat. You know, they sleep upside down."

"How was it?"

"Actually, it was quite unpleasant. I feel lightheaded and hungry and like I might throw up."

"Birch."

"Yeah?" He unstraps himself from the table and groggily steps out.

"I brought you these." I practically throw my jar of Mildred's cookies at him like they're poison or hot coals and I can't wait to be rid of them.

"Whoa." Luckily, Birch catches the jar. Lou's ergonomic coaching must be working.

"They're rosewater almond," I say.

"Sort of like Mildred's ice cream from charades night."

"Yeah. Mildred made them. They're pink from beet juice again. She says hi. Actually she says, '*Bonjour*, sugar dumpling.'"

"Cool," says Birch. "Thanks."

"She also says to brush your teeth like it's going out of style after eating them."

"OK," says Birch, laughing. "I got it."

"OK," I say. I gave him the peace offering after being so terrible and blaming him for Adam and *Crowd Pleasers*, so now I can leave. But wouldn't you know it, Lou's got a new motivational poster hanging on the wall by the door. This one has a picture of penguins jumping from a tall glacier into the ocean with the word COURAGE in capital letters underneath. The quote says:

"COURAGE IS RESISTANCE TO FEAR, MASTERY OF FEAR —

NOT ABSENCE OF FEAR."

— MARK TWAIN

Ugh. Thanks, Mark Twain. Thanks, glacier-jumping penguins. And thanks, Lou, for your motivational posters.

I turn around to face Birch. My mind feels tangled up like seaweed. I try to breathe as deeply as I can. I try to master my fear like Mark Twain says.

"I'm sorry," I say.

I start to turn back around again but Birch is looking at me expectantly, like I've made a pause and not a full stop. I stay facing him.

"Um, there was this volunteer at one of Dr. Flossdrop's pet adoptions," I say.

Birch listens. The way he always listens.

"Anyway, she said that when dogs bite, it's usually because they feel threatened. Like scared that they're going to be hurt, or they're in danger."

When I finish my bizarre dog speech, the only sound left in the room is Lou's television streaming in from the kitchen and the faint buzz of bees in my ears.

"So you were a scared dog, and that's why you bit me?" asks Birch, barely masking his smile about calling me an actual member of the animal kingdom, not just an honorary one.

"Yes. That's what I'm saying. I'm saying sorry. For blowing up at you. I didn't mean it."

Instead of responding, Birch pries the lid off the cookie jar and retrieves two pink mounds. He hands one to me and takes a bite of his own. I do the same. A big sugary, doughy, rosewatery bite. We stand together, eating floral cookies, the sound of chewing added to the room.

"I'm sorry too, for what *I* said that wasn't too sensitive. And I forgive you," says Birch. "Some dogs bark and some dogs bite, and that's just the way it is."

"Ugh. Thanks."

"Kidding. Of course you're not a canine. You're a flower. Zinnia, remember? A flower with bees on her head."

I nod and roll my eyes and nod some more. I finish my cookie. Birch has reminded me why I showed up here the other day — to talk to him about my plan . . . before we saw *Crowd Pleasers* and everything fell apart.

We both sit down on some kind of massage table Lou has like it's a regular bench. My feet dangle, and Birch's touch the floor. I definitely smell peppermint being this close to him again. I look at Birch, and he hands me another cookie.

"Can I ask you something?"

"Hit me," he says, so I do. Softly on his plaid shoulder.

"Ouch."

"Sorry. Are you interested in another secret mission if I tell you what it is up front this time?"

"Hmmmm. That is an interesting question." Birch scoots off the table and rests his elbow on a giant turquoise plastic ball of Lou's. He makes puzzled thinking faces. Then he finally stops stalling and answers. "Yes."

That's it. He says yes. After how I acted. After everything. I guess I should've known he wouldn't hold my bite and growl against me.

"How do you feel about neighborhood action projects?" I ask.

"Big fan," he says.

"And writing an email that uses adult vocabulary?"

"At your service."

I tell him about my plan, which I'm calling *Operation Flora Bomb*. I ask about getting Lou to help us with some shopping and explain Dr. Flossdrop's original tree-planting neighborhood action idea.

"So I guess you didn't need my naturalist expertise to help figure out your bee problem after all," says Birch.

"I guess not. But I still need you for this," I say, which makes Birch's eyes get all sparkly.

When I leave, I get to thinking how Birch and my initials put together make BZ. As in buzz. Which I have to say is pretty weird. But pretty cool too.

24
OPERATION FLORA BOMB

This is it.

I'm sitting at the meadow wearing some frilly pink gardening gloves Mildred lent me. My hood is exceedingly hot and, of course, full of bees, but not for long if today is a success. One frilly pink-gloved hand is submerged in a box of pebbles that I satisfyingly clink together, counting the clinks.

Then I spot Lou trekking toward me. At least, I assume it's Lou because of the athletic pants and great strength he's exhibiting — he's carrying a giant bag of soil, another giant bag of fertilizer, and a huge flat of flowers. The stack is so high I can't see his face. Behind him is Birch, carrying one flat of flowers and some trowels. A canister of water completes his pyramid. Amazingly, nothing topples over. I can't help but feel proud of him.

I remove my hand from the pebbles and wave to Birch. "Over here, Coach!" I yell to Lou, who probably can't see thanks to his stack of supplies.

They amble over and set down their loads. Lou stretches his hands to the sky and his back cracks.

"You finally called me Coach," he says. "Don't think I didn't notice."

"Consider it payment for helping me today," I say.

"I won't consider it that at all. I know the truth," says Lou. He pauses for effect. "You've wanted to call me Coach for years."

"Don't let it go to your head," I say.

For a moment, the three of us stand there. Just when Lou looks like he's about to dive for some push-ups in the grass, Birch says, "Well, let the dig begin!" He rolls up his sleeves and hands me a trowel.

"You mean the bomb."

"Right. Let the flora bomb begin!"

And we do. We flora bomb.

We dig holes. We drop the flowers in the holes. We tug at their spindly roots to help them latch onto the soil. We add more soil and fertilizer. We cover them over and pat down the dirt. We stream a little water from Birch's canister over the base of the stems.

At least Birch and I do. Lou eventually wanders off to do core exercises in the tall grass somewhere.

"My mom told me that studies show people who come in contact with dirt are happier than other people," says Birch. "My mom gardens, and she's really happy."

Knowing Birch, neither of those facts is a shock to me.

I take off Mildred's pink gloves so *my* hands can come into contact with dirt. I haven't really done anything like this since the bean-sprout experiment in fourth grade. I feel a little happier already, just like the studies show. Optimistic at least.

But there's still a whole lot of flora bombing ahead of us before Aunt Mildred arrives — with Dr. Flossdrop and the neighborhood action members — for the unveiling. It's not like a yarn bomb, where you do the work beforehand.

We've only got a fairly measly bed of flowers in the ground so far, and the sun is getting high and hot.

I'm distracted momentarily by a trio of butterflies nosing around the flowers we've already planted. They're tiny ones — two yellow, one white.

And then I see it. Another insect flies nearby. A bee! I hope it's one of my bees.

I stare down that solitary bee while it lollygags around the flowerbed. It ducks into an orange poppy, and I picture it sipping nectar and harvesting fluffs of pollen onto its little legs in there. The way it's meant to. I silently wish for her to tell her friends or siblings or queen or whoever needs to be notified about the pollen buffet.

Birch looks totally absorbed in what he's doing. He's too much in his gardening zone to notice anything as small as a bee. I hope on my own. I telepathically will the other bees to leave too, even though that's never worked before. But this is different. I adjust my hood slightly, opening up a tiny pocket of air in the front. An escape route.

I keep planting, and I can feel sweat droplets in a rivulet down my back and behind the creases of my bent knees. I wipe some sweat from my forehead, a place I can easily reach. When I bring my arm back down, there are more bees lollygagging around the flowers in the ground.

These *must* be *my* bees. I can tell. I know them by now. There's a small stream of air coming from my hood. I can actually *feel* them slowly departing.

Can this really be happening?

I hope they have a good time. I hope they become drunk on floral delight. I hope they all join in the flora bomb as soon as possible and *forever*.

We spend the next hour or so working without talking much. Me, Birch, Lou. I keep my hood on, waiting until the time is right to check if I can take it off completely. If I'm really, truly free.

By afternoon there's an explosion of flowers in front of us. Which is fitting for a flora bomb. The ones I know the names of are lavender, poppies, cosmos, oversized purple daisies, plus my namesake, zinnias. We planted a whole rainbow of them that Birch and Lou insisted we get when we were at the store. The bright gold ones are my favorite.

Even more bees frolic around the newly planted flowers. Like, a whole huge bunch of bees.

I feel lightheaded. Literally.

I slowly bring my hand near my hood. I pluck it off so it falls to my neck. There's no force field feeling. There's no squirm. I tap my scalp, tentatively, bracing for what I might feel there.

I feel . . . hair. *My* hair! My hair that I haven't actually touched — except for wet in the shower — in so long. I'd forgotten what it felt like. It feels like hair! On the bee-greasy side, but still my own wild, curly hair. I pat my head like a beauty contestant who's just been crowned, not quite believing I've won.

Birch is staring at me.

"Wow, I've never seen your hair before. It looks a little like a bees' nest actually," he whispers.

I splatter a handful of dirt on his shirt — plaid, of course.

"Just kidding," says Birch. "I really like your hair. It suits you perfectly."

"Thanks. I like it too. More than I ever knew."

By the hottest part of the afternoon, we're finished. We've even spread pebbles around the top of the flowerbeds so they look fancy.

Flora bomb complete.

Bees gone from noggin.

"That was the best," says Birch.

Of course *best* makes me think of *best ever*, which makes me think of Adam. Adam who isn't here. But that doesn't sting the way it did just a few days ago.

I feel like what Mildred said the day Adam left was true. He had something he needed to do. Something he's great at and deserves. And despite the fact that he kept it a secret from me, I know he won't forget about me in the process. Just like I won't forget about him, even though I'm doing new things too.

It wasn't that he didn't trust me, I realize. I think it was that he had to trust himself. And that meant doing it without me. Looking out over our flora bomb, I understand.

Birch is right. This is my new best ever.

I reach over and give him a high five. His hands are caked with dirt, and his fingers are longer and skinnier than mine, and it all feels just right.

25
UNVEILING

At four o'clock on the dot, a whole bunch of people start showing up. Neighbors, dental patients, Lou's clients. Even the neon-bandana bike-riding guy from the neighborhood is here. The lady who sweeps up trash. The multiple dog walker, some kids on skateboards, and older kids with headphones on.

And NML. I added them to the list of email addresses I gave Birch, the ones from Dr. Flossdrop's neighborhood action list. I decided I didn't want to hide from them anymore.

They're here. They're walking toward us.

"Hey, it's NML!" says Birch.

"Shh," I say. "I mean, yes."

"Hi," says Lupita.

"Hi," say Margot and Nikki.

"Hi," I say.

"This looks really great," says Lupita. She's wearing purple like she always does.

"Thanks," I say. And then silence. I really don't know what to say after that. Awkwardness hangs in the air. I count the number of skinny headbands Margot wears — seven.

Then Birch speaks up to save us.

"I'm Birch, Zinnia's other friend. I wonder if we could all go swimming sometime this summer."

"Sure," they say. It's that easy.

"I've never been in a swimming pool," Birch continues.

"What?" everyone else present says.

Oh, Birch. I'm sure NML will revoke their answer now. But I don't back away from him. Birch was right when he said he's my friend.

"Yeah, I've gone swimming in the ocean up north, but it's really cold. I'd like to try being in water that doesn't give you goose bumps."

NML and I shake our heads like this is the saddest thing we've ever heard. We're doing it all together so it's kind of like NMLZ again.

"You really need to go in a pool," says Nikki. "It's like roller-skating. It's fun to do once in a while."

I glance at her in surprise. I thought NML didn't roller-skate anymore. Maybe they do, though, and the thought of us roller-skating together again someday makes me excessively happy.

Still, I change the subject before Birch can tell us he's never *heard* of roller skates.

"Thank you for the yarn," I say. "I got it. And . . . I wanted to say sorry. I was wrong about you guys turning me in. And I'm sorry about last year . . . the way I acted. I was probably pretty weird."

"You've always been pretty weird," says Margot, but her face is sunny when she says it, so I know she's just teasing me. If she can tease me like that, it means we're really fine.

NML say their goodbyes, and Nikki does a cartwheel as her exit.

I look at Birch.

"The flora bomb worked," I say.

"It was a good idea," he says.

"It was a good email," I say. "Sounded just like Dr. Flossdrop."

"Well, her neighborhood action list is pretty loyal," he says. "And a meadow beautification project is a very popular idea."

"Yeah, there were a lot of signatures on that original tree petition," I say.

Just then I spot Mildred walking toward us with a woman who I can only assume is Viviana. She wears blue-and-white stripes and a wide sunhat and looks like someone who might be learning French.

Viviana and Aunt Mildred each carry one handle of a big bucket filled with bottles of lemonade. They have a slightly confused Dr. Flossdrop in tow. Of course Dr. Flossdrop's wearing all black, except for her white lab coat. And her hair is back in a bun again. And, *of course*, Milkshake wheezes in her arms. But at least it's a healthier wheeze than before. I finally understand what all those people on our walks might see in him. Maybe, just maybe, he's really sweet.

Out here, in this sunny square of the meadow, the air feels as charged as lightning with Dr. Flossdrop's approach. I'm just waiting to hear thunder — or feel rain.

Dr. Flossdrop is about to say something to me when the whole group of people gathered at the meadow starts clapping as though this were the end of a play, and it's time to applaud. They're clapping for the neighborhood action. And for Dr. Flossdrop. After all, as far as they know, this was *her* neighborhood action.

Only Dr. Flossdrop looks confused. She turns to me, and I nod. Her face lights up the way it does when a donation for the library comes in. She points to me and then to the flowers, and I nod again. She gestures toward me in front of the crowd, and then she starts clapping too. Now they're all clapping for the meadow beautification we've done. For me and Birch.

I consider it, but I can't bring myself to do Adam's fancy bow.

Then the clapping dies down, and people go back to chatting. Lou gives me a thumbs-up sign and winks as he leaves the meadow with one of his clients. Before Dr. Flossdrop has a chance to say anything, Mildred says, *"Bravo, bonbons."*

Luckily Birch is the kind of guy who doesn't seem to mind being called a miniature candy. *"Merci,"* he says, which comes as a surprise that makes us all laugh.

Mildred pets my hair. "You look nice not all covered up, my *petit cheri*," she says.

"Wow," says Dr. Flossdrop, taking in the burst of flowers.

I think that *she* thinks I did this just for her. That I'm taking after her in the neighborhood action department. And she's a little bit right. It was nice to do something for her, something she would like. Plus, I figured the city wouldn't object to flowers, especially once they were already in the ground. But I also did it for me. I run my own hands through my bee-free hair. I did it for *all of us*.

"Zinnia," says Dr. Flossdrop, "this is very, very . . . *useful*." She looks so pleased her eyes are actually brimming with tears. The happy kind.

"Thanks," I say. My head feels incredibly light and still and quiet and clear.

But Dr. Flossdrop isn't finished. "It's also delightful," she says. "Which is just as important."

"*Oui*, a work of art," adds Mildred.

Meanwhile, I'm looking at my mother like she's just sprouted wings. Of course, I'm no stranger to peculiar afflictions.

"Looks like your brother isn't the only talent in the family," says Viviana.

Clearly word about Adam's whereabouts has gotten out.

"Thank you," I say before looking at my mom.

Dr. Flossdrop hands Milkshake, who whimpers, over to Mildred, and I give him a friendly scratch behind his ears. Then she comes closer to me. She strokes my hair almost the way Mildred was doing before. Well, more awkwardly, but almost. Maybe she actually notices I'm not covered with a hood anymore too.

"I love you, Zin," she says, so close to my ear that no one else can hear. "Whether you're useful or artistic or totally out of my control. No matter what."

I can't help but beam. These are the most passionate words Dr. Flossdrop has ever uttered that aren't about oral care or neighborhood action. And they're just for me.

Bees
FEAST

We awoke, groggy from bored naps. And to our disbelief, here was our chance. Right in front of us.

While no one had forgotten about the disastrous job Bee 641 had done the first time around, the queen immediately made an executive decision.

"Bee 641 is the only one here with any experience," she said — at which we all scoffed about how dismal said experience was. But the queen continued. "And every bee deserves a chance to redeem herself."

Honestly, we didn't have time to argue. We didn't care about Bee 641 or about our future or about finding a home. There were flowers before us. The kind that actually grow in the ground! We could see the bright circles of their landing pads from the top of the human's head. Landing pads that would lead us to the very things we craved most, despite having resigned ourselves to never tasting them again.

All we could think of was sweet, sweet, nectar.

Our tongues tingled in anticipation.

Meanwhile, if Bee 641 could sweat, her forelegs would've been doing just that. Every filament of her exoskeleton stood on end. Off she went to find a home near this new, miraculous food source. And then, more importantly, off we went to plunder, barely able to wait our turn.

But poor Bee 641. After all that concrete, all that gray, she couldn't help herself. Those beautiful bright colors called to her. Purple especially! Delicious violet! Bee 641 could feel the electricity the flowers sent her way, faintly at first, and then stronger and stronger until she could no longer resist.

Bee 641 thought she could take one tiny slurp of nectar on her way to search for a home, but she couldn't stop after the first slurp. Or the next. Or the next.

It wouldn't have been apian of her to pass up such bounty. She nuzzled shiny petals and cavorted with butterflies. She filled her pollen baskets and dreamed of bee bread. She was so overtaken that none of her five eyes could see straight for hours. Until the moment she finally looked up, giddy, only to see the human packing things up in a way that indicated she was going to leave the area.

Bee 641's giddiness disappeared upon realizing the whole mission was another failure. From her spot on a cosmos petal, she could see nothing nearby resembling a proper abode. Her second chance was shot. She'd squandered it.

Round 'em up, round 'em up! *she heard herself yelling at the foragers.* The human is leaving!

We all came to, euphoric from stuffing our proboscises and pollen-packs. Leaving? We're not staying here with the flowers? *Smiles slowly slipped from our fuzzy faces.*

We have no hive except for her! *Bee 641 implored.*

So we followed, reluctantly, taking sidelong glances at the poppies as we made our way back to the human's head for a heavy-hearted landing.

We had one thing to say to Bee 641: That's it. This time we mean it. You are never, ever scouting for us again.

26
REPEAT

While everyone else is drinking lemonade and looking at flowers, Birch and I clean up, gathering trowels and empty bags of soil and fertilizer.

And then I feel something on my head.

Something foreign, yet familiar.

Let it be bird poop, I think. Please, please let it be bird poop.

But I have a feeling it's not bird poop. I feel another something, and it's unmistakable. I swear I can feel each bee's miniscule set of feet drop anchor.

Noooooooooo!

Birch sees what's happening and grabs an empty fertilizer bag to hold up so no one *else* can see.

It doesn't take long before all trillion of the bees are back in place. My head squirms and purrs and itches. I put my hood up and head down.

I was so close to this all being over. So close.

Birch pats my shoulder, I'm sure thinking this whole entire thing was a fail.

But maybe it wasn't.

I have another idea. I've learned something today. And it's that everybody needs to feel at home. Even if it's not exactly, perfectly the kind of home you always thought you wanted.

27
HIVE

It's sunrise at the meadow, and I'm all alone.

The bundle in my arms is pretty unwieldy. I guess I should have expected that from a never-ending scarf. It's more like a skinny blanket for the world's biggest baby.

I unfurl it and lay it down on the grass. It's a colorful snake, a rainbow dragon.

Then I remove my hood and wait to see what happens.

The bees leave again. They bound among the flowers, just like yesterday. If this works, I'll never feel their weight again. But I still have to find out if this *will* work.

Beginning at one end, I wrangle the scarf, coiling and tucking, pushing and pulling. I feel like a magician with one of those super-long chains of handkerchiefs. I wrap and wrap, and eventually it resembles an ombré, egg-shaped object with a hole in the bottom — like a beehive, only brightly colored and made of yarn.

I pull loose some bits of thread from the top and tie them around a skinny water pipe over by the flora bomb. The fuzzy oval now dangles there over the flowers.

Then I wait. Again.

Soon, enough time has passed that the sun is right over the poppies we planted yesterday. The sky is as orange as they are. Slowly, gradually, it fades to pale pink.

The bees are fixated on the flowers. Maybe they'll never notice or care about that thing hanging nearby.

But then, one of the bees leaves a flower and zooms toward my scarf pod.

Other bees begin to follow, first a sparse line of them and then more and more until they've formed a long, thick, wiggly streak. The bees are a gray stripe through the cotton candy sky. They're headed, it seems, in the direction of the yarn hive!

And then their streak stops.

They hover together in a cloud. It's like they've convened a meeting in midair.

It's possible they're going to change direction.

But they don't.

As though linked in a chain, the bees gather together by the fuzzy globe. Then they fly inside, disappearing from sight.

I'm free.

Something like joy bubbles up through my chest to the top of my head. I imagine the bees rooting around the yarn and wonder what the new hive is like for them — not that I plan on ever getting close enough to find out.

I remove my hoodie completely. I'm wearing a charcoal-gray tank top underneath, and the sky is now light blue with a huge yellow sun. I can abandon the hoodie until fall. I feel like throwing it on the ground and asking Dr. Flossdrop to buy me a new one, maybe an actual color this time, but I tie it around my middle so as not to be wasteful.

I spin in a circle, twirling and fist-pumping the air.

I'm not the only one here, though, and I'm not the only one fist-pumping the air.

Birch stands in the meadow over by the crosswalk, binoculars around his neck. He walks closer, and I can see faint circles around his ocean green eyes. He's still fist pumping and spinning around. We both are as we meet dizzily in the middle of the meadow.

"That appears to be a knit beehive," says Birch. "And the bees appear to like it. Quite an ingenious idea, Zinnia Flossdrop." He bumps my arm with his plaid elbow.

"How did you know I was here?"

"I was up already, listening for the dawn chorus of birdsong, and I heard you leave. Your front door makes kind of a *whoosh* sound."

"Yes, it does."

"I take back everything I've said before. What just happened is actually the coolest thing I've ever seen," says Birch.

"Me too. It's our secret," I say, which makes Birch smile like a great blue heron just landed on his head.

I'm going to miss Birch when he leaves to go back to Redwood City for school. But maybe he'll come back next summer. And we could keep in touch. Maybe we can do a yarn bomb together before summer is over since the flora bomb was so successful. Lou's TV. Or one of Dr. Flossdrop's dental chairs. I think she would be open to that now.

And since my never-ending scarf is finally finished and is a beehive, put to good use, I'll make Birch a scarf. I'll stop when it's regular-sized. He can wear it when he gets cold after soccer practice in the fall. I'll have to find just the right color, green-blue and shimmery like the ocean.

Bees
HOME

Just at the moment when we'd given up hope again, when even regurgitating nectar to one another couldn't lift our mood, we got another go at the feasting site.

Nobody said anything about electing a scout or any such nonsense. We knew that would come to nothing. We just went about our business, filling our pollen sacks, and slurping nectar as quickly as creaturely possible. It was the only thing we could do. Take some small pleasure in flying and in the iridescence of rarely seen petals. Prepare for the rest of our days before us, trapped on the human's head and headed for nothingness, by stockpiling supplies.

But then, a tiny wind fluttered Bee 641's antennae. She focused. She took in air through all her breathing holes. She heard a small voice inside her. And she listened.

Bee 641 was lured up and away to a far corner of the garden. There before her was something soft that smelled . . . familiar.

Infused with some kind of supernatural confidence — despite her track record — Bee 641 got the others' attention. She tread the air before them. She turned around. And then she began to dance. *It wasn't the moonwalk or the robot or the worm. Oh no, it was a dance of our very own invention. The waggle dance.*

Bee 641 wiggled and waggled like no bee has ever wiggle-waggled before. She'd never done it, and yet, right then, she was doing it. Figure-eighting her heart out with waggle panache.

First we ignored her. Oh, there's 641 again, *we said.* She never lets up.

But then something stirred inside our midguts. We believed once more in Bee 641 and in the order of things. Against all logic, we followed.

And Bee 641 brought our colony home.

An assembly was called. A verdict reached. A decree issued. We were to stay put.

Who needs bears and forests when we can have a full day's work, the life for which we're destined, right here in this garden? *said the queen.*

And we, of course, concurred.

It was a new era. We could finally make honeycomb. The queen could begin laying eggs again. We immediately detected that her perfume had returned. It smelled sublime. And it meant that all was going to be well.

A retirement ceremony was held for Bee 641. A formal apology was issued from the colony. She was given an honorary title — Bee 641, Extraordinary Hive Scouter Emeritus. Plus, she would receive her very own supply of royal jelly to enjoy every day at teatime, in the queen's royal chambers, newly established in our exceedingly cozy hive.

It was a glorious occasion. I should know. Bee 641 was me.

28
DISPATCH

Birch and I are at Scoops. Where else would we be? It's going to be the hottest afternoon of summer so far.

It's been two days since the yarn hive, and I'm still bee-free! Plus, it's just about time for *Crowd Pleasers* to come on. As much as Dr. Flossdrop and I have come to a new understanding — and even though she's excited that Adam is on the show — she's still not about to get a TV herself. She says she'll watch clips of Ace's performances online.

I'm hoping today I actually get to eat my ice cream at Scoops. Finish the whole thing this time. But after my third bite of lime-kiwi sherbet swirl, Adam's girlfriend walks up to the table where we're sitting. Her dark hair is up in a ponytail, and she's wearing cut-offs and the Starving Artists Movers T-shirt with the collar all big and hanging off one shoulder to reveal the bird part of her tattoo.

She seems just like the kind of girl my brother belongs with.

"I have something for you," she says. She hands me an envelope filled with doodles, which I immediately recognize as Adam's, and walks away.

I shovel in one more bite of sherbet, fully tasting its sweetness and zing, before I open it.

Zin,

I know how hard it must've been that I left. I had to try something big to see if I could make it as an artist without Dr. Flossdrop stopping me. I'm sorry I didn't tell you. That was the worst, but I had to do this on my own. I hope you'll understand someday.

You inspired me. Your rattlesnake yarn bomb was really amazing. I have so much to tell you, and I'm sure you have a story or two for me.

Say hi to Mom. Bonjour to Aunt Mildred. And tell them both I'm making time to floss.

I miss you,

Adam

A story or two — ha! I think, running my hands through my hair. If he only knew the story of my summer.

But oddly enough, I feel more at home with Dr. Flossdrop and NML and even myself than I did when Adam first disappeared, despite the fact that he left me. Maybe even because he did.

People at Scoops start shushing each other. The show is about to start, and I tuck Adam's letter in my sock. Birch and I adjust our chairs to face squarely toward the screen.

"Hey, Birch?" I whisper.

"Yeah?"

"Thanks."

"For what?"

"For not giving up on trying to be my friend."

"Well, bird-watchers have to be patient and determined," he says, holding out his yarn-bombed binoculars. "And interested in strange birds."

I laugh and so does Birch, his green eyes twinkling.

Just then the show's opening rolls, and Ace parades on camera in face paint and a mime outfit. He's wearing silver boxing gloves this time, and I can't wait to see what he's going to do with them.

My heart goes fluttery, and I have the urge to cheer for my brother. Birch and I lean forward so we won't miss anything.

Because this is going to be good.

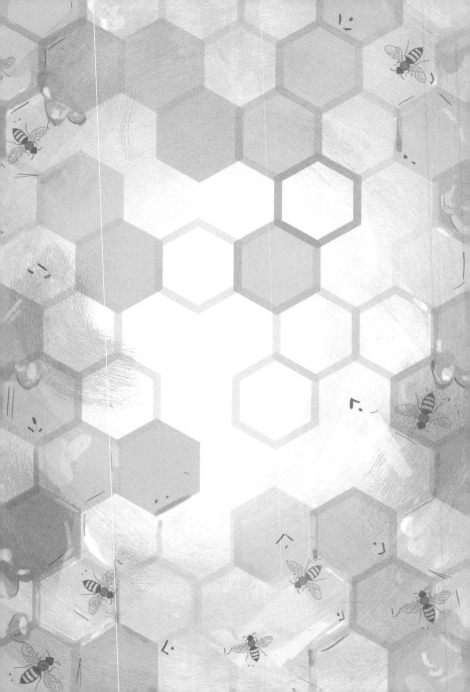

Acknowledgements

A writer's dream is to have someone like your work and take a chance on it. Thank you to my agent, Rick Margolis at Rising Bear Literary, for doing that and more.

Thank you to my super talented editor, Alison Deering, for turning this manuscript into a book, and for making it so much better in the process. And thanks to everyone at Capstone: Tracy McCabe, Kay Fraser, Shannon Hoffman, and Beth Brezenoff, as well as to Lauren Forte for her copyediting and to Laura K. Horton for so beautifully illustrating the cover. Many thanks also to Courtnay Walsh, April Roberts, and Geogia Lawe.

And much appreciation to the following people for their help and kindness along the way:

Edan Lepucki, for guidance years ago on a version of this manuscript when it was something else entirely. Susan Hawk, for thoughtful insight into my first tries of this story as middle grade. Martha Alderson, The Plot Whisperer, who is an invaluable resource for any writer and a wonderful human being. Margaret Wappler, for her Writing Workshops Los Angeles class and feedback on key parts of this story. Dee Romito, Jennifer Maschari, and Casey Lyall, mentors extraordinaire, as well as my debut buddies in our Facebook group. Alethea Allarey, for generous knitting expertise. Anything I got wrong in that department is on me. Emily Arrow, for camaraderie. I'd write you a song if I could. Katherin Patsch, for tea, walks, wise advice, and so many celebrations. Bonnie Eng, for friendship, enthusiasm, and collaboration. Gabrielle, for listening and understanding, and for being someone I continue to learn from and admire. My fourth-grade teacher, who read novels aloud to our class at Singapore American School. I think I contracted lice from the bean bag chair I sat in, but it was worth it. My English teacher senior year of high school, who believed in me in a way I felt no one ever had before. The students I taught middle school to years ago. Reading alongside you better acquainted me with a body of literature that now feels like home.

And finally, Todd, to whom this book is dedicated. Support isn't a strong enough word. Thank you for your confidence in Zinnia and me all these years. Having a partner who is understanding, accepting, and also wildly creative is no small treasure.

About the Author

Danielle Davis grew up in Singapore and Hong Kong and currently lives in Los Angeles. She has an M.A. in literature and creative writing and has had the privilege of teaching English to middle school and community college students. Now, she reads and writes and enjoys volunteering with literacy organizations. *Zinnia and the Bees* is her first novel. You can visit her online at www.danielledavisreadsandwrites.com